She was trapped!

"Please!" The plea escaped her on a husky groan as she twisted around with the intention of pushing him away from her.

"Please, what?" His dark eyes lowered to watch the way her hands trembled against his broad chest. "You know what is happening between us, Cassandra." He sighed impatiently. "We are violently attracted to one another, so stop trying to fight it, for it only adds to the agonizing frustration. The outcome is inevitable."

MICHELLE REID lives in Cheshire, England, dividing her time between being a full-time housewife and mother, looking after her husband and two teenage daughters and writing. She says her family takes it very well, fending for themselves until she "comes up for air," though she's not sure which they find harder to put up with, being cleaned and polished when she's in a housekeeping mood, or being totally ignored when she's absorbed in writing and tends to forget they're alive! She has a passion for fresh air and exercise, which she gets at the local tennis club.

Books by Michelle Reid

HARLEQUIN PRESENTS
1440—A QUESTION OF PRIDE
1478—NO WAY TO BEGIN
1533—THE DARK SIDE OF DESIRE

HARLEQUIN ROMANCE
2994—EYE OF HEAVEN

MICHELLE REID

Coercion to Love

Harlequin Books

TORONTO • NEW YORK • LONDON
AMSTERDAM • PARIS • SYDNEY • HAMBURG
STOCKHOLM • ATHENS • TOKYO • MILAN
MADRID • WARSAW • BUDAPEST • AUCKLAND

Harlequin Presents first edition October 1993
ISBN 0-373-11597-0

Original hardcover edition published in 1992
by Mills & Boon Limited

COERCION TO LOVE

CHAPTER ONE

'ARE we nearly there, Cass?'

Cassandra Marlow sent an encouraging smile to the hot little girl who was dragging heavily on her hand. 'Not far now, poppet,' she said. 'Just to the top of this hill and around the corner.'

Eyes so dark that they looked black behind their thick sooty lashes stared dolefully up the dusty street baked glaringly white by the hot Italian sun, and a long sigh shook her little body. 'That seems an awful long way to me,' she complained, conveniently forgetting how happily she had skipped *down* the steep hill that same morning, too eager to get to the beach to think about the long walk back from it. 'I wish we were back home. It isn't so hot in Fulham.'

No, thought Cass. But danger lurked in Fulham. The kind of danger a five-year-old couldn't begin to understand. A danger which had dogged their footsteps for a whole year now. Carlo Valenti was back on the prowl there.

Which was why, on what Cass honestly acknowledged had been a burst of bitter defiance against the dratted man, she had decided that *they* would spend the next few weeks in *his* home town! Working on the theory that, with him in London, San Remo must be about the safest place on earth for them to be at the moment!

She only hoped that he remained true to form and stayed put in London for the two weeks he usually put aside when believing himself to be hot on their trail.

'Why couldn't we stay in one of those nice big hotels down by the beach?' Terri wanted to know. 'Then we wouldn't have to walk so far every day to play in the sea.'

'Because it needs money to stay in one of those posh places down there, Terri,' Cassandra explained, adding rather drily, 'And money is something we are rather short of, I'm afraid.'

Coming here at all had put a rather nasty hole in the precious nest-egg she had stashed away. To have paid the prices those big hotels down in the bay were asking would probably have seen it off completely!

'We never do have enough, do we?' The child sighed. 'Not since my mummy went away...'

Cass's heart twisted at the simple yearning in the child's voice, her green eyes clouding over on thoughts of her sister. Yes, Liz had earned enough for them all to live on. But she'd had to work like a dog to get it.

God, Liz, she thought sadly, I miss you.

And she did, all the time. Until Terri's arrival on the scene, she and her sister had only had each other. Orphaned at an age not much greater than Terri's now, the five-years-older Liz had been the closest thing Cass had ever known to a mother. But being fostered into different homes had made it difficult for them to see each other, and it wasn't until Cass began her two-year course training to be a nanny that she was able to live permanently with her sister. Liz was already a top photographic model by then, living the kind of glamorous life which was totally alien to her quieter, much younger sister. But she'd taken Cass in without hesitation when she'd learned she was going to train in London, allowing her to share her plush Kensington flat while Cass finished her course.

Not that they had seen much of each other, Cass ruefully recalled, with Liz always seeming to be flying off to some glamorous location or other. And, on qualifying, Cass herself had landed a fantastic job taking care of a film star's two small children, which took her off to Los Angeles for twelve months while he filmed his latest block-buster.

Coming back to England had heralded drastic changes in both their lives. It meant she was suddenly the nanny to her own niece while Liz went back to work. The car crash last year had ended that successful arrangement. And all of a sudden it wasn't Liz, Cass and Terri, but just Cass and Terri, hunted, by a man who hadn't even acknowledged the existence of his own child while Liz had been alive!

God, she despised Carlo Valenti.

'We're here.'

'Oh,' Cass blinked, surprised that they had finished the final part of their uphill trek without her being aware of it.

Just across the road stood the peeling white walls of Giuseppe's Garage, where the modern petrol-pumps looked out of place against the aged and crumbling building, in which was the accommodation their two-week holiday had afforded them. The small garage lay just off the busy *autostrada* that ran right around the Riviera Di Pontente from Genoa to the border with France, and collected a steady amount of customers from those who left the motorway here in San Remo. But it was siesta time now so the road was quiet, and as usual Giuseppe was lazing in his chair beneath the shade of a battered old awning, and he waved and smiled as he noticed their approach. 'You have a nice day?' he enquired genially.

'Lovely, thank you,' Cass called back as they crossed the road towards him.

'The *bambina* looks hot,' he observed. 'It is a tiring walk back from the beach, is it not?'

'Much easier going down!' Cass returned, sending him a warm smile which died the moment she saw how thoroughly his eyes were exploring her long-legged figure covered only by a thin vest-top and brief shorts.

'You are protecting that delicate skin of yours against our hot sun, I hope, *signorina*,' he murmured, lazy eyes lifting to take in the purity of her naturally pale skin framed by the rich copper glow of her long loose hair.

Cass made some coolly polite reply, then excused them both and ushered Terri around the side of the garage to where a flight of concrete steps led up to their small apartment. She didn't want him getting any ideas about her. Being a woman alone with a child made her vulnerable enough. Giuseppe might be in his mid-fifties, fat and balding, but his eyes certainly knew how to roam. The point was, did his hands know how to do the same thing?

'He looked at you funny, Cass,' Terri innocently confirmed her aunt's own cynical thoughts as they mounted the steps.

'Did he?' she murmured absently, pretending not to have noticed. She didn't want her niece feeling insecure here of all places. She'd already experienced enough of that in her young life.

'He looked at me funny too,' the child added ingenuously, bringing Cass's smile back because she was well aware of the odd couple they both made—she with her milk-white skin that had to be caked in sun-block cream if she wasn't to turn the colour of a strawberry, and Terri with the kind of natural dark skin of a native from these parts, when, in truth, neither of them had set foot in Italy until two days ago.

But it was that same rich Mediterranean colouring which sometimes, when Cass was feeling particularly vulnerable, made her heart squeeze in recognition of where it had come from. She had spent long hours worrying about it, swinging between a real fear that she might be doing the child a grave disservice keeping her ignorant of her Italian roots, and a fierce certainty that she was doing the right thing whenever she thought of her sister and how badly Carlo Valenti had treated her.

'Mmm,' Terri sighed in relief as they entered the delicious coolness of their small apartment, the closed shutters having kept out the worst of the afternoon heat.

'Mmm, indeed,' Cass agreed, thrusting her resentful thoughts aside in favour of a long, cool shower to rid both herself and her niece of the salt, sand and sun-cream which was stuck to their skin.

By eight o'clock, Terri was fast asleep in one of the two narrow beds which took up most of the room in the cramped studio apartment, and Cass had taken herself out on to the small balcony to watch the sun go down.

One of the advantages of staying so high up was the wonderful view she had of the bay beneath her. The dying sun had turned the rippling ocean into a lake of dancing fire, and the tumble of red-roofed buildings below them glowed warmly against the dying sun, high-lighting the complicated maze of winding alley-ways and narrow staircases which made up the delightful Old Town of San Remo. Further down, she could just make out the exotic row of canary palm trees lining the famous Corso dell'Imperatrice, and beyond them was the marina where the private yachts moored side by side, their tall masts bobbing gently on a lazy sea. And anchored further out in the bay were several larger yachts, all big and white and luxurious. She had seen the exclusive hotels down in the town which must draw the wealthy cruisers in. Big old elegant places built in another era for the kind of wealthy clientele who still frequented them now.

The Valenti Grande was just one of those luxury hotels.

'Rolling in it,' she murmured cynically to herself. 'Simply rolling in it.'

'Don't ever let money be your lure, Cass,' Liz had warned her once, the bitterness of disillusionment clear in her voice. 'It means nothing without honour and self-respect. And those greedy for it honour and respect nothing.'

Carlo Valenti had no honour. His affair with her sister had lasted just long enough for him to get her pregnant, then he'd left her flat. Cass would never forgive him for that, never!

Her only confrontation with Carlo Valenti had come via the telephone several weeks after her sister's funeral, when she was up to her eyes in packing cases and worrying what she and Terri were going to do without Liz to provide for them. There was little to nothing left in the bank. Living a double life had come expensive for Liz, Cass had soon discovered. Only the chosen few knew about Terri. It was the way of the advertising business. Babies were bad news, so when it became known to her agents that Liz was pregnant they sent her on a long vacation, and called it exhaustion through overwork. After Terri was born and Liz had exercised her figure back into shape, she went back to work, and Terri was kept firmly in the background. The trappings of such a glamorous job cost money—lots of money— more than a stunned Cass could have dreamed. Their nice Kensington flat was leased, not owned, the furniture along with it.

In short, she and Terri had little to nothing to live on except for the tiny inheritance her sister had had the foresight to put to one side in the eventuality of anything tragic happening to her. But that was only enough for them to live on if they did so frugally. And it was the immediate problem of where they were going to live that was filling Cass's mind the day the telephone rang and that deep, barely accented voice came imperiously down the line.

'My name is Carlo Valenti, and I wish to see my daughter,' he announced. No preamble, just those words exactly.

Cass felt the first quivers of alarm for Carlo Valenti shiver down her spine. 'What daughter?' she replied, not because she was being sarcastic, but because she was stalling for time to think.

Sarcasm or not, he ignored it. 'I am catching the next flight out of Genoa for London, and should be at your flat by the evening,' he informed her. 'Make sure you are there to receive me.'

'For what purpose?' she demanded.

There was a pause—one which made the fine hairs at the back of her neck tingle, then the voice came back slowly and carefully, 'For the purpose of bringing Teresa back here to Italy to live with me, of course.'

They left Kensington that same afternoon, and had been on the move ever since, Cass taking jobs wherever she could to help supplement their small nest-egg, eyes always on the look-out for any suspicious characters who may be watching them. The moment she got an inkling that they were being observed, or heard of someone asking questions about either of them, she upped sticks and moved on. Their last stop having been Fulham, where, in actual fact, they had managed to stay the longest—a whole month and a half!

Then she'd seen it in the paper—the photograph of his sleekly handsome face and the announcement that Carlo Valenti was in London and planning to stay for some time. Business, they called it, naming some juicy project which would attract a man of his mercenary calibre. But Cass knew better. He'd found out she was in the Fulham area, and was on the prowl again. The man must have been furious that his arrival had been noted by the Press.

Well—— Cass smiled smugly at the steadily darkening sky above her—she'd certainly put one over on him this time! While he sat stewing in his expensive London hotel suite, waiting for his detectives to track her down yet again, she was basking in his very own Mediterranean haven!

Justice, she called it.

By the time their two weeks were up here, they would be boarding a plane which would take herself and Terri up north instead of back to London, and right out of Valenti's reach. She'd got a job. A real job as a full-time nursery assistant in a pre-school nursery attached to the infant school Terri would be attending.

Cass was a Londoner, born and bred. He wouldn't think of looking for her anywhere north of the Watford Gap—just as he wouldn't think of looking for her here! She'd covered her tracks well. No one knew where she had gone to, and neither did anyone know where she meant to go next!

The mosquitoes were beginning to bite. Cass swatted one as it landed on her arm, and went back inside, smiling to herself as she pulled the shutters closed. She was going to enjoy the next two weeks without having to look over her shoulder all the time. And that, she told herself firmly, was a promise!

A promise she found very easy to keep as the days drifted lazily by with no sign that Carlo Valenti had discovered their whereabouts. Between them, she and Terri developed a routine which simply consisted of spending most of the day down on the crowded beach before coming back to the apartment in time to shower and eat a light meal before the child fell happily exhausted in to bed. Terri's skin grew more tanned and healthy as time went on, and Cass was pleasantly surprised to find her own skin taking on a soft golden hue with the careful help of a high-factor cream.

'I wish we could stay here for ever and ever,' Terri sighed contentedly several days later as they were coming back from their day on the beach.

'So do I,' Cass smilingly agreed, realising with a jolt that she actually meant it! She might hate and despise Carlo Valenti, but she had learned to love his beautiful San Remo over this last week.

Giuseppe was busily filling the petrol tank of a beautiful creamy white Ferrari when they arrived around the corner which brought the garage into view. A tall dark-haired man wearing a pale blue shirt and buff-coloured casual trousers was leaning against the shiny bodywork of the car chatting lightly to Giuseppe as they waited for the tank to fill. The garage owner glanced up and saw them, and sent them his usual smiling greeting.

'Ah,' he called. 'Miss Marlow and the *bambina*! You had a nice day, heh?'

They had paused beneath the shade of a huge old olive tree to check the road before trying to cross it. The afternoon heat was oppressive today. Terri was pulling heavily on her hand as usual. A bee was buzzing annoyingly around the tangled mass of Cass's bright red hair. And Cass was more interested in getting out of the heat than anything else as she lifted her gaze to smile at Giuseppe just as the man with the white Ferrari swung around to face them. Cass glanced absently at him then away again, the female in her vaguely registering his lean, dark Italian good looks. Then something went click in her brain, and she stiffened, the ice-cold feel of dread slewing everything inside her to a shuddering, grinding halt.

The world stopped moving. She forced herself to look at him again, praying desperately that she was wrong and knowing wretchedly that she was right. She had lived for too long with that face etched on her memory to mistake it when she saw it. The way he wore his straight black hair swept negligently away from his lean-boned face. His eyes, dark dark brown and as hard as pebbles. The long smooth line of his Roman nose. His mouth, thin and cruel with a tendency to wear a sardonic curl to one corner. She knew every detail of that face as intimately as she knew her own, had spent hours staring at it via the photographs she had ripped out of various newspapers. Hating him, despising him for what he had done to her sister.

And it was most definitely him. Carlo Valenti.

She couldn't move, couldn't breathe, the cold, hard breath of fate holding her trapped in the horror of her own making, and for long, slowly moving seconds they just stood there staring at each other across the width of the dusty road, his own shocked amazement at finding her here in his own San Remo of all places registering in the astounded expression on his face.

Giuseppe murmured something in Italian, his tone matching his puzzled frown at the suffocating tension suddenly assailing them all.

'Cass?' Terri whispered anxiously, moving closer to her as the strange tension got to her also.

'It's all right,' she murmured, but her voice was low and thick, too restricted by the horror she was experiencing to give much comfort.

The child's movement made Carlo Valenti's dark lashes flicker, and he shifted his gaze down to the little girl. Instantly something blazed into violent life in him, and sent the air wrenching from Cass's lungs on a pained whimper.

It was recognition, instant and possessive.

'My God,' he breathed at last, his stunned gaze lifting back to Cass. 'My God. It is you.'

Yes, she thought emptily, it's me all right. Living in a fool's paradise. 'You were supposed to stay in London for another week at least,' she heard herself say stupidly.

'Business demanded my early return,' he informed her as though it were her God-given right to know.

Cass even managed to smile at it, acknowledging the way both of them had been caught completely unarmed by the unexpectedness of the situation. He smiled too, causing her to catch her breath as those eyes so like Terri's glinted ruefully at her.

The world began to move again, birds twittering lazily in the shaded branches of the tree, the bee buzzing, the light breeze kicking up the dust from the road. The sun shone brightly down on the bodywork of the Ferrari, and Carlo Valenti relaxed suddenly, leaning back against the car and folding his arms across his chest.

'Well, well, well,' he drawled, getting a hold of himself far quicker than Cass could manage. 'So the lamb has walked right into the lion's lair.'

'I'm no lamb for the slaughter, Mr Valenti,' she disclaimed, lifting her chin to defy a taunt she knew held more than a little truth to it. 'Don't make the mistake of comparing me with my sister.'

Liz had been the meek little lamb. She had allowed this man to use her, then leave her flat when the going got tough. Cass was made up of an entirely different stuff.

'You are quite right, of course,' he entirely agreed, using those eyes, narrowed against the sun, to slice over her in derisive contempt. 'There is no comparison. At least Elizabeth could give the appearance of being an angel when necessary, while you, Miss Cassandra Marlow, look and are, nothing but a——'

'Don't you shout at my aunt Cass!' All of a sudden Terri was thrusting herself on the scene. 'And my mummy is only an angel 'cos she's dead!' The shrill statement wobbled a bit, and Cass tried to gather the angry little girl to her, but she was having none of it, pulling away so that she could stand free, legs planted firmly apart, hot and angry face turned up to challenge this stranger who had dared to deride her mother's name and shout at her aunt Cass all in one breath. 'I don't like you!' she shouted across the road at him. 'You look like somebody I know, and I don't like you!'

A damning recognition of herself in him, Cass noted on a violent shudder.

He had begun to straighten slowly the moment Terri squared up to him, his eyes fixing in real fascination on his hostile daughter. 'I am sorry you think that, little one,' he murmured quite gently, 'because I mean neither of you any harm.'

Terri ignored him, turning to Cass and holding out her small hand. 'C'mon, Cass,' she instructed firmly, 'let's go,' almost as if she were the adult and Cass the child. 'We don't have to talk to him if we don't want to. He's bad, I just know he is.'

Out of the mouths of babes...thought Cass grimly as she took the proffered hand but made no attempt to move from the spot. Unlike Terri, she wasn't so naïve as to believe he would let them walk away just like that.

'Now why should you think that, Teresa?' There was an odd thickness to Carlo's voice that forced Cass to acknowledge that he was finding this no easier than she was. 'You don't even know me, so how can you decide if I am bad or not?'

Terri frowned at this piece of good logic, her free hand going up to rub her dusty face. 'You're trembling, Cass,' she mumbled. 'He frightens you, doesn't he?' she said, then burst into tears.

Cass wasn't surprised by the sudden outburst. But she knew Carlo Valenti was. Terri's bouts of bravery were usually followed by tears. Still struggling to gather her scattered wits together, Cass bent to scoop the poor little girl into her arms. 'It's all right, poppet,' she murmured soothingly, 'Carlo isn't bad.' She used his first name deliberately, hoping the familiarity would help ease Terri's fears. Whatever else Cass wanted, she did not want the child living in fear of anyone. 'He's just surprised to see us here, that's all.'

'What did I do?' Suddenly he was standing right in front of them, big and lean, his handsome face taut with concern. 'What did I say to hurt the child?'

'Nothing,' she replied flatly, thinking, It's me who's done the hurting by trying to put off the inevitable. 'You—snarled a bit, that was all, and Terri is very protective of me.' She hugged the sobbing child closer. 'If you'll excuse us, Mr Valenti, I think I'll take her inside so I can——'

'No.' The refusal came hard and gruff, any hint of softening in the man gone in that instant. 'No,' he said again. 'This time there will be no clever escape, Cassandra Marlow. No chance to slip by me. You will both come with me right now,' he announced, 'or the child comes with me alone. The decision is entirely up to you.' And, before Cass realised what he meant to do, he had reached across and plucked the sobbing child from her arms.

'Oh! You can't do that——!' Drenched in sudden panic, she made a flailing attempt to grab Terri back from him, one set of trembling fingers curling around the rock-solid muscle of a male forearm while the others held on for dear life to a fistful of Terri's T-shirt.

The child began yelling at the top of her voice, her little fists pummelling into any place she could hit on the hard-packed frame now holding her in an effort to get free. Giuseppe stepped forward, concern clouding his brown face. 'Signore...' he began uncertainly.

A barrage of Italian hit the garage owner's ears which sent him stumbling back several steps, his gaze sliding over to Cass with a look which accused her of murder.

'What did you tell him?' she demanded over Terri's shrill cries.

'Exactly who it is I hold in my arms,' he bit out harshly, grimly holding the struggling child while her desperate blows continued to rain all over him. Eyes like black onyx impaled Cass with a bitter challenge. 'Are you prepared to deny that this child is *my* daughter?'

On a gasp, Cass glanced sharply at Terri, hoping she was too busy yelling to have overheard what he had just said, knowing it was no use denying his angry challenge when people only had to look at the two of them together to know immediately where Terri sprang from. For all Cass's strong blood-tie with the child, she could not say the same thing. There wasn't an ounce of Marlow visible in her sister's daughter.

God, she asked herself wretchedly, what have you done, coming here?

'Please give her back to me!' she begged him. 'She's frightened enough as it is, without you making her think you're going to run off with her!'

'In the car,' he said grimly. 'You can have her back when we are all safely in the car.'

'But...' Fear was crawling between the fine layers of her skin, and she glanced huntedly around her, looking for someone—anyone—who would come to her rescue. But there was only Giuseppe standing there, staring at her as though she were a criminal. 'M-my—our things...' she mumbled helplessly. 'I—I have to get s-some things from the flat...'

'Get in the car, Miss Marlow,' Carlo Valenti instructed immovably, ignoring everything else.

Beaten, Cass turned and walked across the dusty road, and climbed into the low-slung car, dizzily aware that there was precious little else she could do at this moment.

He handed Terri to her the moment he had struggled in beside her, face set as he slammed his door shut. The engine fired, and with a growling surge of power they shot forwards, the accompanying sound of the central locking system clicking into place sending a cold shiver shooting down Cass's spine.

'Fasten your seatbelt!' he barked at her.

'With Terri in this state?' she choked. The poor thing had driven herself into such a sobbing frenzy that she was even fighting Cass now!

'Her name is *Teresa*!' Carlo grated. 'Please use it instead of that awful slang version. I dislike it intensely!'

'When I want your opinion, I'll ask for it!' Cass threw back, struggling to fasten the stupid seatbelt around herself while hanging on to a near-hysterical child. 'I can't *believe* you made a grab for her like that!' she added shrilly. 'Have you no sense?'

'The point needed to be made... *Dio*!' he muttered, bringing the car to a sudden halt, then twisted around to snatch the seatbelt out of her fumbling fingers to fasten it himself. His hand inadvertently brushed against Cass's breast, and it didn't take an idiot to know she wasn't wearing anything beneath her thin T-shirt.

Cass in turn sucked in a sharp breath, shocked by the hot *frisson* that skittered over her skin. Her cheeks warmed. He cursed, and Terry wailed all the louder because the tension inside the car was so great that it was in danger of exploding all around them.

'I hate you,' Cass mumbled thickly.

'The feeling is entirely mutual,' he clipped, grimly settling himself back in his own seat.

'I hate you too,' hiccuped another voice.

'If I were you, I would be too busy hating myself for
making such an awful noise,' Carlo informed his hostile
daughter.

His unsympathetic scorn had the effect of stopping
the tears, and Terri sat up on Cass's knee so she could
stare at him with more curiosity than fear now. 'I still
don't like you,' she informed him bluntly.

As if against his own advice, his hand jerked up to
gently touch the child's hot and tear-stained cheek. 'No,'
he murmured gruffly, 'I don't suppose you do.'

'Cass doesn't like you either.'

'No,' he sighed, letting the hand fall away to return
his attention to the car, setting them moving again with
his expression even blacker.

'Did my mummy like you?' Her in-built perception
took both adults' breath away.

Carlo's foot slipped off the accelerator, making the
powerful car jerk and shudder. 'Yes,' he answered
through tautly clenched teeth, 'your *mamma* liked me.'

Terri frowned, trying to puzzle that one out. She had
grown up being used to a united front. Where Liz loved,
Cass and Terri invariably loved also, and vice versa. This
man seemed to be an exception to the rule.

'Angels watch over the living,' she suddenly announced, why, Cass didn't even try to understand. 'My
mummy won't let you hurt me or Cass. If you try, she'll
send you to the devil!'

'Terri!' Cass sighed, scolding her for what, in actual
fact, could be a great comforter to herself if she could
only believe in it.

As if sensing she had gone about as far as both adults
were going to let her, Terri put her head on Cass's
shoulder and closed her eyes, one set of little fingers
playing idly with a salt-stiffened lock of flaming-red hair.

'She is very outspoken,' Carlo murmured after a while when the steadiness of the child's breathing said that she had fallen asleep.

'She has a mind of her own, and likes to use it——' Cass was instantly on the defensive '—so don't think you can win her over with your false Italian charm the way you obviously did her mother!'

'I want my daughter, Cassandra Marlow,' he stated grimly, answering the angry challenge in her voice.

'You never wanted her when Liz was alive.'

'That is a lie,' he growled, turning his head to scowl at her. 'If your sister had——'

'Keep your excuses for Terri,' Cass cut in tightly. 'I have no wish to hear them.' She lifted her own gaze, as green as glass and twice as cold, to clash contemptuously with his. 'In my eyes, Mr Valonti, there are no excuses worth listening to that can justify a man's deserting a woman pregnant with his child!'

CHAPTER TWO

THEY continued their journey in hard silence after that—
Cass sitting stiffly beside Carlo, her heart throbbing with
a deep and burning malevolence for the man, while he
drove with his handsome face closed to everything, increasing the speed of the car to send them flying along
the road, through the busy town and out on the other
side, past his very own Hotel Valenti Grande without
even sparing it a glance.

They hit the cliff-road which connected San Remo with
Genoa, the car speeding by the spectacular views on
either side of them with all the powerful grace of its
famous reputation. It was a full ten minutes before they
turned off the main road and on to a narrow by-road
that took them zig-zagging up a hillside drenched in
afternoon sunlight. But it was only as they reached the
peak of the hill and Cass saw what was waiting for them
on the other side that she showed any reaction whatsoever to the scenic beauty of the drive.

Before them opened up a ravine-like valley the likes
of which she had never seen in her life before. Eden in
hell, she named it drily as her senses were bombarded
by the sheer drama of the view below them.

Narrowed almost to nothing at either end and thickly
lined with trees, the valley opened into a wide, fertile
basin in the centre cut almost in half by a thin river which
threaded its silvery path along the valley's full length,
snaking around clumps of heavy leafed trees, and bab-
bling over bleached white rocks as it went. A house stood
on the other side of the river, its white-washed walls

blinding in the afternoon sunlight. Single-storeyed and built on four wide spreading wings around a central courtyard, it was surprisingly modern and more in the Spanish hacienda style than the old stone-built *casa* you would expect to find in a place like this. Yet it possessed picture-postcard qualities, set as it was in such lush surroundings. Cass just managed to glimpse horses grazing in a field to one side of the house and cattle in another before the road took them beneath a canopy of tall fir trees.

'Trust you to live in a place like this,' she muttered, knowing somehow that this whole valley must belong to him.

'I will not apologise for my wealth, Miss Marlow,' he threw back grimly.

But will you apologise for the way you treated my sister? she wondered, then scowled because she did not want his apologies. It was blatantly obvious that this man had enough money to keep a hundred unwanted children in luxury!

They were dropping sharply downwards now, the sunlight seeping through the high tree-tops dappling the ground all around them. He had slowed down considerably as soon as they'd begun their descent, the steep, winding road demanding his full attention, and Cass found herself turning to study him.

He really was the most outstandingly attractive man she had ever seen, she reluctantly confessed as something inside her did a flip and a dive in response to the sheer male virility he exuded. She observed his features, strong and proudly Roman, his straight black hair combed carelessly back from a high, intelligent brow which led to the long, thin, arrogant nose. His mouth was slim and straight, wearing a slight sneer which went with his contemptuous character. His dark brown eyes were hooded at the moment, lost beneath blackly frowning brows as he concentrated on his driving, long, blunt-ended fingers with short well-kept nails lightly hooked around the leather-bound steering-wheel, a heavy gold wedding-ring on his finger catching her eye as the sun burned on to it.

'You're married!' she gasped in appalled accusation, making Terri jerk in her sleep.

He lanced her with a withering look. 'Widowed,' he clipped, then added deridingly, 'before I met your sister,' the hardness of his expression warning her not to push that line of discussion any further.

She turned her face away, having no intention of probing into his past. This man's life was his own. The only part of it she was interested in was where it encroached on her own life and Terri's. Then, perversely, she found herself wondering what the late Mrs Carlo Valenti would have looked like.

Beautiful, no doubt, perhaps even a member of the Italian aristocracy, with the same kind of inbred arrogance and sophistication that oozed from him.

They came out of the trees on to the valley bottom, where the road took them between two lines of loose walling trailed by heavily blooming flowers which added charm to an already enchanting scene. They crossed the river via a narrow stone bridge, and drove up to the deep veranda at the front of the house, where another Ferrari was parked, a bright red one this time, gleaming spotlessly in the afternoon sun.

Carlo cursed softly when he saw it, his hard mouth tightening even more. 'Stay there,' she was told as he opened his door, and Cass stared balefully at him as he unfolded his long frame out of the car and came around to open her own door.

But the moment he bent to take Terri from her she hugged the sleeping child closer. 'I can manage,' she clipped, struggling out of the car without his help. There

was no way she was going to let him get his hands on
Terri again. He had all but kidnapped them, frightened
Terri into a fit of hysterics, and terrified herself! He may
have them in his power at the moment, but that was all.
She and Terri were still a pair, and he the unwanted
outsider.

'Carlo!' Surprise echoed in the new voice which broke
into the tension eddying around them, and they both
spun around to see a woman step out from the shadows
of the deep veranda and come gliding down the steps
towards them.

'Hello, Sabrina.' He found a smile, but it was forced.
Obviously he didn't like being caught red-handed ab-
ducting two females! Cass thought acidly. 'What are you
doing here?'

'Am I not always welcome in your home, *caro*?'
Taking her cue from him, the woman replied in English,
her tone awash with all the seductive confidence of one
who knew herself to be very welcome. 'But you were
not expected back for another week, at least.'

She was exquisitely beautiful, Cass noted, of
Elizabeth's age and ilk, with that same glossy finish she
had watched her sister apply each morning before she
left for work. Tall and reed-slender, Sabrina's body
swayed sensually in smooth fluid movement as she came
towards them.

'Business,' Carlo explained. 'I had urgent business to
attend to in Genoa.'

Completely ignoring Cass's presence, Sabrina walked
right into his arms, sliding her hands around his neck
and arching her body against his so that the points of
her breasts brushed against his chest, making him laugh
softly at this blatant coquettish display as he bent to
place a kiss on both silk-smooth cheeks.

'It is good to have you home, *amore*,' Sabrina murmured huskily, her long red-tipped fingers stroking the silken hair at his nape. 'I miss you so when you go away.'

They had to be lovers, Cass decided as she stood there, beginning to burn up with resentment at being made to await their pleasure while the sun blazed down on her uncovered head and Terri grew heavier in her arms with each second that passed by.

She gave an impatient sigh, wondering cynically if Carlo Valenti would even notice if she just climbed back into his car and drove away, his attention was so captivated by the lovely Sabrina!

The sound brought his head up, though, his eyes narrowing on Cass's contemptuous expression.

'Goodness me,' the Italian beauty drawled, 'you have taken to bringing home waifs and strays, Carlo?'

Cass flushed, cringing inside at the open disdain in the other woman's tone. This is all I need, she sighed inwardly as she was made suddenly and uncomfortably aware of how scruffy she and Terri must look to the silk-sheathed Sabrina. Sending Carlo Valenti an accusing glare, she hid her discomfort by making the most of shrugging Terri's dead weight into a more comfortable position.

'Here, let me.' Cass jumped, startled once again to find him suddenly standing in front, and, for the second time, he took her by surprise by plucking Terri out of her arms and folding the child into his own strong embrace.

The other woman was standing glaring at Cass with the kind of hostility that said she did not like being upstaged by a scruffy waif and sleeping stray. Then Terri stirred in her sleep, and Sabrina's attention was suddenly caught by the hot little face turned up to the bright sunlight.

'So,' she let go with a soft gasp, looking just a little shaken beneath the mask of superior derision she had been wearing, 'this is the child you have been searching so long and hard for, Carlo.'

'*Si,*' he answered huskily, locking Cass's throat up on a jealous bank of tears as his mouth brushed the sleeping child's brow, dark eyes softening to look so tender that it made her want to scream and kick in much the same way Terri had done earlier.

'Go home, *amante*,' Carlo ordered suddenly. 'As you see, I have guests, and they are tired; I have no time to entertain you today.'

'But Carlo,' Sabrina cried in outright dismay at the way she was being so summarily dismissed, 'I came here especially to see your *mamma*!'

'Then I will offer my mother your apologies, and she will surely arrange another visit for you at a more convenient time.'

With that, and without a second look at the other woman, he turned towards the house, obviously expecting Cass to follow him. And with a helpless shrug she did so, finding she had enough of the bitch in her to enjoy the stony look on Sabrina's lovely face as they left her standing there with Carlo's absent, '*Ciao*,' ringing in her ears.

The light was dim inside, the air deliciously cool after the fierce heat of the afternoon sun. Cass followed him across the tiled floor and through another door which brought them into the central courtyard where brightly blooming flowers trailed in glorious profusion over white-washed walls. Bougainvillaea, honeysuckle and pretty star-shaped clematis all vied for space. Huge terracotta pots stood on the cobbled ground, spilling with bright red and pure white geraniums, and the air was leaden with the scent of them all.

Carlo led the way around a small central fountain where a stone cupid sprayed diamond-studded water into a lily-covered pond, then through another door which brought them into yet another spacious hallway.

'My own private wing,' he informed her as he moved across the hall to fling a door open wide before stepping back to allow Cass to precede him inside.

She did so reluctantly, afraid of what might be waiting on the other side.

'It is not a prison cell,' he drawled, reading her mind. 'It is a suite of rooms, which you and Teresa will use during your stay here.'

'Who said anything about us staying?' she challenged on a last ditch attempt to assert herself, but she was trembling with alarm, and she sensed he knew it.

The room was large and square, furnished with chic and modern elegance in soft tones of creams and green. The walls were lined with creamy fitted furniture, and a double bed covered in cream satin stood between two pairs of soft-green satin-draped french windows. Not even in Liz's expensive flat was she used to this kind of stylish luxury—nothing overstated, but just simply if expensively done.

'Teresa's room opens off this one.' Carlo nudged by her, carrying the child across to a half-open door where once again he waited for Cass to precede him through it.

There was no sign of satin in this room, she noted as she stepped inside. Instead the whole was furnished in bright childish cottons of sky-blues and summer-yellows. Carlo laid Terri down on the pretty lemon duvet-covered bed, where a big pot-bellied, sleepy-eyed grey rabbit sat high on the pillows above the child's sleeping head.

'Is there anything we can do to make her more comfortable?' he asked, frowning down at the disreputable state which was his daughter.

Cass moved to stand beside him, her face automatically softening as she took in the wild disarray of jet-black curls tumbling around a dirt-smeared face. A brief glance at the man beside her told Cass that he hadn't escaped his share of dirt on his expensive shirt, and she gained some small satisfaction from knowing it.

'I'll remove her sandals, that's all,' she said, bending to the task. 'She won't sleep long.' The poor thing would be hungry, having missed out on their lunch to stay longer than usual at the beach today.

Straightening again, she almost cried out as her shoulders made contact with his chest. She hadn't realised he had moved to stand right behind her, and she spun around to face him warily. He was staring at her, the colour of his eyes so dark that they looked black beneath the sweeping curve of his thick lashes. A strange warmth went washing through her, prickling along the surface of her skin, and she jerked nervously away, her mouth trembling a little as she pushed around him and made quickly for the other room. The last thing she needed was to become physically aware of him; she had enough to contend with coping with the other powers he had over them right now.

'Now we talk, Mr Valenti,' she demanded grimly when he joined her. Her chin was up, her face pale but determined as she faced him.

Pausing in the process of drawing the door to Terri's room to, he sent her a narrow glance. 'Take my advice,' he suggested, ignoring her demand. 'Take a shower and a short siesta; by then perhaps tempers will have cooled and the shock of our surprise meeting will have worn off enough to allow anything we have to say to each other to be less—abrasive.' He began striding across the creamy tiled floor, every line of his body smooth, graceful, infuriatingly arrogant.

Her eyes followed him in angry disbelief. 'You expect me to calmly take a nap after the way you've just abducted us?' she choked.

'I expect you, Miss Marlow,' he informed her coldly, 'to wait on my convenience—as I have had to wait on yours for the last twelve months!'

'No!' She was beside him in an instant, grabbing his arm to stop him from opening the door. 'I want to know how long you intend keeping us here,' she insisted.

His top lip did a sardonic curl. 'You, Miss Marlow, can leave here any time you wish to do so,' he informed her with insufferable indifference. 'But Teresa stays with me.'

'No way.' She shook her bright head. 'And you have to be living in cloud-cuckoo-land if you honestly believe I'll even consider leaving her in your dubious care.'

He didn't like that; his long back stiffened, and he glared at her down the length of his arrogant nose. 'Do you live well with your conscience, Miss Marlow,' he drawled, 'knowing how you have deprived that child of her rightful father?'

'Do you mean the father who was quite happy to live with his conscience, believing her gone before she had a chance to survive?' she threw right back. 'You bet I can, *signore*!' she jeered. 'My sister left Terri in my legal care, but you have done your level best to make that job impossible for me—and, by the way things are going,' she pushed on hotly when he went to interrupt, 'things are only going to get worse! Because I will *not* give up my guardianship of Terri to you. And neither you, nor your money, or even your bullying tactics, will make me. You can drag me through every court in Europe without winning this one, Mr Valenti, because I know, you see,' she told him, green eyes as hard and cutting as glass. 'I know how you paid my sister to have Terri aborted.'

'That is a lie!' he barked, fury leaping into his eyes. 'And you, Miss Marlow——' he pointed a stiff warning finger at her '—would do well to be careful what you say to me until you are in possession of all the facts, and not just those your twisted sister fed to you!'

'Don't you dare try blaming Liz for your own sins!' she cried.

'I dare,' he said harshly, 'because I knew her for what she really was, and not what you in your stupid blindness believed her to be!'

Cass sucked in an angry breath and held on to it before even daring to answer. 'My sister's only folly in life,' she breathed out eventually, 'was falling for a dirty rat like you! Don't you dare touch me!' she choked as he took a jerky step towards her.

'Touch you?' he ground out, reaching out to do just that, and grabbing her by the upper arms with hard fingers. 'I ought to beat the living daylights out of you for speaking to me like that, you vicious-mouthed little cat!'

'What's the matter, *signore*?' she taunted recklessly, eyes alight with a matching aggression, the bright colour of her hair no mere quirk of nature—Cass had a temper that could erupt like Mount Etna if riled to it, and this man was dangerously close to making it do that right now. 'Has the truth hit a raw nerve?'

'Why, you——!'

For a horrible moment, Cass thought he was going to hit her. Certainly, one of his hands left her arm to clench into a white-knuckled fist. Then he thoroughly shook her by muttering something ungodly beneath his breath, and pulling her against him so that he could slam his angry mouth down on to hers instead of the clenched fist.

All that hot pulsing anger boiling between them converged and converted itself into something far more dangerous. It shot through them both like pure electricity, fusing their mouths together and setting their bodies shaking as furiously; he ground her lips back against her tightly clenched and tingling teeth.

'You bastard,' she whispered when at last he let go of her, leaving her trembling so badly that she could barely stand.

'Something I am not, but my daughter certainly is through the crazy machinations of your sister.' His mouth tight with contempt, he grabbed hold of her wrist. 'Since you have managed to force this discussion to take place now, you will come with me, and we will get a few important points straightened out before your vile tongue gets you into further trouble.'

'I can't leave Terri here alone!' she protested when he began pulling her across the room towards the suite door.

He didn't even pause. 'Someone will come and sit with *Teresa*——' he almost thrust Terri's proper name down her throat '—and the child will be quite safe here since there is not a person in this valley who would harm a single hair on her head. Whereas you, Miss Marlow——' he all but yanked her through the door and into the hallway '—I could quite cheerfully strangle myself and think the prison sentence worth the trouble!'

Stalking them both across the hall and in through another door, he threw her angrily away from him and turned to close and lock it, making sure she noticed how he pocketed the key. Then he strode across the room to pick up a telephone.

Cass looked away from him, her hair falling untidily around her face as she concentrated on rubbing her throbbing arms where his fingers had bitten into her. She would have bruises there tomorrow, she thought angrily, listening to him bark out instructions to whoever was on the other end of the phone. She wanted to rub her bruised mouth, too, but refused to give him the sat-

isfaction of knowing how much that kiss had hurt her.
So she lifted her head and scowled at him instead, hating
him with her eyes, trying to hold down the desperation
wanting to quiver through her body. That burst of violent anger between them had alarmed her more than
she dared admit even to herself.

'Why do you want Terri, anyway?' she demanded the
moment he came off the phone.

'She is my daughter,' he clipped, 'and I have more
right to her than you do.'

'She's my niece,' Cass came back, still rubbing at her
bruised arms, 'and I will always love her more than you
could ever do!'

Something swept across his face, a look gone before
Cass could analyse it, but, whatever it was, it seemed to
drain the anger right out of him, and he sighed, starting
towards her with slow, heavy strides.

'Let me see.' He took hold of her wrist, extending her
arm for his inspection, mouth tightening when he saw
the reddened finger-marks already forming bruises on
her pale flesh. 'I apologise for this,' he said. 'I don't
usually put bruises on women.'

Because they probably don't dare answer you back,
Cass thought ruefully. 'Y-you don't need to do that.'

She tried to pull away from him, but he wouldn't let
her. His fingers were brushing lightly over the reddened
patches on her arm. Then he grimaced to himself over
something, eyes lowered so that his dark lashes fell in
two thick silky curves across his lean cheeks. The fingers
stopped stroking and curled around her arm instead,
measuring the reddened finger-marks with a gentle
grimness.

'If I am so disdainful of human life, then why have
I spent the last twelve months trying to meet my
daughter?'

'I don't know,' she shrugged. She had never been able to understand why he had pursued them so relentlessly when he hadn't given a care about Terri while Liz had been alive! 'You didn't even come to Liz's funeral, did you?' she accused him, pulling her arm from his light grip. 'Even in your capacity as one of her past employers, you could have at least shown your face there. You met her because she was doing a promotion for your hotels!' Her green eyes condemned him with a look. 'And she was good at her job, good enough to bring the punters flocking to your exclusive resorts, no doubt.' A wretched sigh shook her, and she wrapped her arms around her body in an attempt to still the aching grief that always swept through her when she thought of her sister. 'It was weeks before you bothered to contact me about Terri,' she went on thickly, 'yet her name was plastered all over the papers alongside Liz's when they reported my sister's death. You must have known she was your daughter!'

'I was away,' he said. 'In South America, visiting my sister and her family there. I did not hear about Elizabeth's death until I returned—and also discovered that she had not terminated her pregnancy as I believed she had done,' he added grimly.

'So what is the difference now you do know your original plan was not carried out? I read your letter, Mr Valenti,' she put in quickly when he opened his mouth to defend himself.

'Enclosed, cheque,' it had begun with all the businesslike manner of a man with no heart whatsoever, then went on to lay so many insults at her sister's feet that Cass could still feel sick just remembering them. All of them had implied that Liz was one of the lowest forms of life itself. 'Under the circumstances, I would prefer it if we never meet or speak again,' the letter had coldly finished.

She shuddered. He saw it, and sighed impatiently. 'When I paid that cheque over to your sister, I did so because I believed the deed already done!'

'My sister told you so?' she challenged.

'Yes,' he nodded, holding her hard look steady.

Disbelief glowed in her eyes. 'Then why,' she posed, 'if that was the case, is Terri sleeping peacefully at this very moment, in your house?'

'Because your crazy sister lied to me!' he snapped.

'No.' Cass refused point-blank to accept that, her expression so totally ungiving that he shook his head, as if trying to clear it.

'It is useless trying to have a fair and constructive discussion with you, isn't it? You are so completely biased that you wouldn't listen to me even if I forced my side of events down your wretched throat!'

'Terri was and is,' Cass stated grimly. 'If you didn't care one way or the other five years ago, then you can't expect me to believe you really care now.'

Muttering something beneath his breath, he spun away from her, a hand going up to rake in frustration through his silky black hair. Then, on a sudden spurt of energy, he strode back to the desk. It was only then that Cass realised they were standing in what could only pass as his study. The room was lined with books and packed with the computerised trappings of a rich businessman. Sitting down in the chair behind the desk with a bunch of keys dangling from his fingers, he unlocked a drawer and pulled it open to withdraw a thick manila file, which he slapped down hard on the polished top.

'W-what's that?' she asked.

His eyes pinned her with the kind of grim intent one used when hell-bent on killing someone else's illusions. 'This contains everything I need to drag your sister's name and her reputation through the gutter if you make it necessary,' he said. 'But there is one item in particular I want to show to you which——'

'You're lying,' Cass cut across him, not even alarmed by the threat. He could have nothing damning on Liz. He was just bluffing. 'Liz's life—before and after you—was so clean it squeaked. Try again, Signor Valenti,' she derided, fine brows arching in polished-copper contempt.

He sucked in a sharp breath, and Cass gained the impression that he just wasn't used to having his word challenged. 'I have the evidence—the irrevocable proof—that your sister was nothing more than a low-down——'

'*No!*' Mount Etna erupted with no warning other than that one volcanic negative, and Cass was hurling herself across the room in a frenzy of uncontrollable rage. She would not—could not—listen to him, of all people, defile her sister!

She made a grab for the file, intending to rip the lot to shreds without deigning a single glance at a single sheet of his lying proof! But he stopped her.

'*No!*' His denial was just as explosive, the hand lying on the file pressing down with all his weight as he shot to his feet and stood glaring at her across the width of his desk. 'You don't get your destructive little hands on this, Miss Marlow. This,' he bit out threateningly, 'contains my guarantee that you will give me full and complete guardianship of my daughter!'

'And just the very fact that you can have such a file makes me certain you are not the man to have control of Teresa!' Sucking in an angry breath of air, Cass placed her palms flat on the desk and sent him a look which said that the very sight of him made her sick to her stomach. 'I *won't* hand Terri over to a man who has the power to ruin her mother's memory! I *won't*, Mr Valenti, give you the time of day while that file——' she sent the manila folder a scathing glance '—remains a threat to Terri's love for her mother!'

Silence followed that. And Cass stood, shuddering in the aftermath of her own explosion, watching the dull flush mount his handsome face before it paled to a shaken whiteness, and knew—knew—she had at last managed to cut the arrogant devil down to size.

Carlo was staring at the file, his hand still protecting it from Cass's destructive intentions. Then slowly, and in a way which held her breath locked inside her chest, he picked it up and replaced it in the drawer, locked it securely, then straightened himself up to his full and imposing six feet odd height, and lifted his eyes back to hers. 'Nevertheless,' he said—no anger, no sarcastic, 'Miss Marlow' in fact, with no emotion whatsoever, 'you will do exactly as I say, or lose Teresa the hard way. And be sure,' he added levelly, 'that, if that is the course you decide to embark upon, then once I win—and I will win, I can promise you that—you will never be allowed to step within a hundred miles of your niece again.'

Acceptance that he meant every word sent Cass stumbling back a step from the desk. 'Then God help you, Mr Valenti,' she breathed, appalled at the depths he was willing to stoop to get his own way. 'Because if you honestly believe that the end justifies the means in this case, then you are wrong. And if Teresa ever finds out how you were prepared to crucify her mother to gain control over her, then she'll hate you for it. Hate you until the day you die. And that, Mr Valenti,' she finished grimly, 'is my promise to you.'

With that, and while he stood there rendered immobile by her flat-voiced vow, Cass turned and walked away, going to stand by the locked door, chin up, head high, tears of anger washing her eyes.

'Does that mean you are prepared to do as I ask?'

Her disgust of him pulsed in the very air separating them as she said quietly, 'It means, Mr Valenti, that I want you to unlock this door so I can remove myself from your contaminated presence.' Green eyes challenged brown to take exception to her contempt, and for a moment she thought he would, his jerky movement enough to put her on her guard.

Then the eyes were hooding over again, and he forced himself to remain calm despite her provocation, a hand going into his pocket to find the keys as he walked smoothly towards her.

'You are on my territory now, Miss Marlow,' he reminded her as he reached around her to place the key in the lock, 'and I don't need the permission of a British court to keep Teresa here. I just do it. No mud-slinging— I simply kick you out of my valley and leave you to do battle with the Italian courts. Which means you having to find the time and the money to do it rather than me.'

Cass shuddered as the cold wind of truth wafted over her. But she refused to let him know it, turning to meet that challenge with all the bravery in her aching soul.

The key turned in the lock, and he opened the door, stepping back to allow her to leave. Cass did so with her head held high, refusing to say another word.

CHAPTER THREE

TERRI was sitting up in bed when Cass entered the room. Clutched to her bosom was the big grey rabbit, and she was staring round-eyed between its two floppy ears at the large homely woman who sat chatting away to her in unintelligible Italian, and whose round face was wreathed with smiles.

'Who is she?' Terri asked curiously, seeming not in the least bit upset that she had woken in a strange bed in a strange room with this strange woman sitting beside her. 'Can't she speak English?'

'I don't know,' Cass said calmly. 'Why don't you ask her?'

So she did, hands clasped firmly around bunny's fat belly, eyes about as round as eyes could get. 'Do you speak English?' she enquired like any seasoned tourist.

The woman burst into a peel of laughter, thoroughly enjoying what she saw as a huge joke. 'A leetle,' she said, squeezing finger and thumb into a half-inch measure of her English ability. 'I Maria!' she then proudly announced.

Terri looked at the woman, then at her aunt, and informed her blandly, 'She's Maria,' as though Cass's own intelligence didn't stretch as far as her own. 'I'm Terri,' she informed Maria importantly. 'And that lady there is my aunt Cass.'

'Ah, Teresa, eh?' Maria repeated expectantly, sending Cass a smiling nod of acknowledgement.

'*Terri!*' the child corrected impatiently.

39

'No, no, no,' Maria shook her jet-black head as she heaved her incredible weight out of the chair. 'Teresa—*Teresa*!' she insisted, and bent to plant kiss on Terri's cheek before waddling from the room with her happy laughter still shrill on her lips.

'She's nice!' she exclaimed, and, to an already emotionally tattered Cass, it was like having her only ally turn on her. 'Do you think she knows that horrid man?'

'No doubt.' Cass quelled the desire to smile in triumph. Maria might have won favour in Terri's eyes, but Carlo Valenti was still right out in the cold as far as his daughter was concerned. 'Since this is his house, and that is one of his beds you're sitting on, I should think she knows him very well.'

'Oh.' Not sure she liked the idea of that, the little girl let her eyes go on a curious scan of the room. Cass watched her with the ache in her heart turning to a throb. She looked so sweet sitting there like that, cuddling the great big rabbit, her little face all brown eyes, and the mop of unruly black curls tumbling in all directions. It was as though all that Italian breeding in her had suddenly leapt into startling life in the bright, gay luxury of the room. Big eyes moved and paused, moved and paused, taking in everything and revealing nothing.

'Had a nice nap?' Cass asked lightly when it became clear that Terri was not going to make a single remark about the room.

Terri didn't answer, flicking her a questioning glance instead. 'Where's that man?' she asked. 'I'm hungry. Do you think he'll feed us?'

'Oh, I should think so—if we can make ourselves presentable enough, that is,' she added, running a rueful eye over the child's disreputable state. 'How about a bath?' she suggested.

Terri shuddered. 'Aw, no, Cass!' she wailed predictably. 'I don't want a bath!'

With a threatening growl which set the small child giggling as she scrambled out of the bed and ran, Cass gave chase, letting the child run off some energy before catching and scooping her up in her arms to haul her off to the bathroom, unaware of how their playful laughter rang out beyond the closed suite door and into the room opposite, where Carlo Valenti sat behind his desk, his face carved in deep, still lines of thought.

The bathroom was big, stylish and inviting, with the same mixture of cream and green as in her own allotted room. A huge sunken bath held pride of place in the middle of the tiled floor, and the moment Terri saw it she changed her mind about a bath. Incredulous at the sheer size of it, she knelt at the side to watch eagerly the water gushing out from concealed taps set in the deep basin wall.

By the time she was stripped of her clothes and ready to jump in, the bath was full, and, with a gleeful squeal, she landed fearlessly in the middle of the clear tepid water. Ten minutes later, and Cass had joined her, clothes and all, when a splashing contest had already drenched her anyway. And for the next half an hour they were just aunt and niece again, sublimely content with each other.

But the problems which faced Cass were never far away from her mind. And neither—she soon found out—were they from Terri's.

Wrapped in soft towelling robes they'd found hanging behind the bathroom door, one a bright sunshine-yellow, the other plain white, Cass was kneeling in front of Terri, drawing a comb through the child's shiny wet curls while all around them hung their wet clothes, dripping on to the fancy bathroom floor.

A small clean finger came up to trace a gentle pattern over Cass's cheek. 'Who is he?' Almost as though she knew the truth was going to rock her little world, Terri put the question with a deep and throbbing reluctance.

Cass swallowed, the tears backing up behind each other. So, she thought heavily, this is it. The moment she had been dreading for a year now.

Did she lie, or did she tell the truth?

'Who would you like him to be?' she fielded, knowing she had shied away from the answer the child deserved.

Small shoulders lifted and fell in an uncertain shrug, eyes the colour of dark chocolate, intent on watching the finger now busily tracing Cass's throat. 'He said he was my daddy, didn't he?'

So, Cass thought as her heart dropped sickeningly to her stomach, she had heard him claim her outside Giuseppe's garage. Cass had suspected as much. Terri so rarely missed anything going on around her. Damn you, Carlo Valenti! 'Well...' concentrating fiercely on the little girl's silky curls, Cass struggled for an answer '...if, let's say, he is your daddy, then would you be— too disappointed?'

The finger reached the deep 'V' in the robe where moisture still clung to the honeyed gold of Cass's skin. 'He—he doesn't like me,' she said, her pouting mouth so vulnerable that Cass drew the little body close.

'Oh, but he does, darling!' she huskily assured, the tears hot in her eyes. 'He loves you so much that he's been trying to get to meet you for a whole year now, only—only...' she swallowed, and willed herself to finish it '...only I wouldn't let him,' she admitted.

There, she thought wretchedly. She couldn't come nearer to the truth than that!

'Why?' Terri stared at her in surprise.

'Because I'm selfish,' she said, and dragged her tongue from the cleaving roof of her mouth. 'Because I was greedy enough to want you all to myself. And because I was afraid that you may not like him, when really I should have left that decision up to you, shouldn't I?'

Smiling through the strains of her own distress, Cass was despairingly aware that almost every word she had said hit more at the truth than she'd actually ever dared admit to herself. Part of her flight from Carlo Valenti had been a personal flight because she needed Terri almost as much as the child needed her. But her hatred of the man deepened further at his forcing her into having to say these things. Because she knew, as surely as night followed day, that, if things were in reverse, he would not have made the same sacrifice for her. And it had been a sacrifice, of all those memories she held so dear of Liz.

But, Liz or no, Carlo was Terri's father, and if the child wanted to accept him as that then there was very little she or anyone else could do about it.

'I'll always love you best, Cass!' the dear child vowed, as if she knew what was going around in Cass's mind, and wanted to reassure her. 'Mummy first, then you, then—him. If I decide to like him, that is,' she tagged on with a frown which revealed her own confusion. She had not forgotten the rude way he had snatched her from Cass's arms earlier. 'And—anyway,' she added off-handedly, 'he might not want me to love him. So we'll have to wait and see...'

Wait and see, Cass repeated bleakly to herself. How many times had she deflected Terri's questions with that phrase? 'How do you fancy combing the wet tangles out of my hair now?'

As a diversion tactic, it worked like a dream. But, as Cass sat cross-legged on the bed while Terri knelt behind her drawing the comb gently through her hair, her mood was heavy. From the moment she had looked across the dusty road outside Giuseppe's garage, and accepted that the man with the white Ferrari was indeed Carlo Valenti, she had feared that her time with Terri was drawing to an end.

The light knock at the suite door several long minutes later brought both females out of their personal engrossment. The sound was a mere slap at convention before he entered.

He had showered too, his dark hair combed wetly away from his lean shaped face. He had changed into a fresh set of clothes, the white loose-fitting shirt tucked into the slim waistband of a pair of casual trousers. He looked clean and alive, his presence alone seeming to shift the atmosphere in the room from the harmonious to the tense with nervous expectancy.

Closing the door behind him, he paused, his eyes narrowing on the two of them sitting on the bed with their shiny faces and guarded expressions, one so dark it threw the other into pure ethereal relief. A nerve twitched in his jaw, and something in his gaze as it rested on them made Cass quiver inside.

Terri was the first to break the stillness, climbing down from the bed to go and stand squarely in front of him. 'Cass said you'll feed us if we're clean,' she announced with her usual bluntness. 'So, we're clean.' She spread her small hands in what was a child's version of sarcasm. 'But we've got no clothes to put on 'cos you wouldn't let us get them from Giuseppe's.' She was doing it deliberately, testing him out with the insolent tone. 'And Cass has to wash the others in that big bath, so we can't get fed anyway!'

'There are plenty of clothes bought especially for you waiting in the drawers of your room, Teresa,' Carlo informed his daughter.

'My name is Terri,' she corrected. 'And that's not my room,' she denied. 'And those aren't my clothes in the drawers either. They belong to some other little girl, but they're not mine. Who do they belong to?'

Carlo threw Cass a sharp look. She stared balefully back. You're on your own in this one, *signore*, that look told him. I've done all I'm going to do to help you.

Lashes so long and thick that they made his eyes look deceptively sleepy flickered then lowered as he shifted his gaze to her mouth. All at once she felt the pulsing reminder of a brutally issued kiss burn against her lips, and quickly lowered her eyes from him, appalled that he could offset her so easily.

'They belong to my daughter,' he informed the waiting child.

Terri took a moment to absorb this, then said in her usual blunt way, which hid a lot of the real feelings which went on inside her, 'Do you love her?'

Oh, Terri, Cass thought wretchedly as she watched his hard mouth soften into a gentle smile.

'Does that room look as though it was made for a little girl who isn't loved?' he replied.

Terri just shrugged. 'I dunno,' she mumbled. 'I've not had a proper look at it yet.' Which was an outright lie because she had taken more than a 'proper' look at it.

Carlo hesitated a moment, as if unsure just what to do next, the lines about his long Roman nose starkly pronounced, revealing the real tension going on inside the man. Then he held out a hand towards her, the gesture tentative, like a man who was making his first approach to an uncertain animal. 'Shall we both go and take a look now?'

Terri looked at the hand, long-fingered and darkly tanned, then at his face, smiling still and nowhere near as hard as it had looked to her outside Giuseppe's garage. Then she was looking back at the hand again, and her own small one twitched before slowly, reluctantly almost, coming up to settle in his. Cass watched his fingers close, and it felt as if thick steel bands were closing around her chest. She looked away, tears burning in her eyes, unable to take any more as jealousy, the likes of which she had never experienced in her life before, ripped right through her.

'Cass?' Terri called to her.

She wet her dry lips, blinking fiercely before turning her head again. 'Yes?' she said huskily. Carlo's eyes were intent on her, and she knew he hadn't missed her pained response to this first voluntary move towards him by his daughter.

'You come too.' Terri held out her other hand, her small face set in a stubborn line.

It was Cass's turn to hesitate, not because she wanted to deny the little girl her support at this crucial moment, but because that earlier look from Carlo Valenti had made her uncomfortably aware of how naked she was beneath the brief white robe, and her hand went to clutch at the lapels in an unconscious give-away of her feelings, which made him smile knowingly.

'I think, *caro*, it may be a good idea if you and I explore the room next door while your aunt looks through the cupboards in here to see if there is anything she may like to—borrow.' He didn't make the same mistake of calling them Cass's clothes, as he had done with Terri, but the implication was certainly there for her to pick up on if she dared to.

He was staring at her curiously, and Cass knew he was puzzled by her passive attitude in all of this. She was puzzled by it too; but she refused to let him see that. Instead she gave Terri an encouraging smile which sent the child off towards the other room with her hand tucked firmly in her father's.

Cass remained where she was, heart heavy as she listened to them talking to each other as they explored Terri's bedroom. Then the fear that he may get back here before she had done something to make herself look respectable sent her sliding off the bed and over to the long bank of cupboards, finding, to her surprise, just about everything a woman could need in the way of clothes, from casual summer outfits to exquisite evening gowns the likes of which Cass had never owned in her life.

This wasn't right. None of it was right, she frowned as she sent her eyes along a long row of light cotton day dresses that she knew, even without taking one out and studying it, would fit her as if they'd been bought exclusively for her.

And there was the rub, she acknowledged. Just as the room next door had been designed specifically for Terri, this room and all its contents were here for her. What was he actually playing at? she wondered as she quickly selected a pale blue sundress and searched out a pair of skimpy cotton briefs from one of the drawers before making for the bathroom to change.

It couldn't be, could it, that he wanted her to stay here as well? Had always intended it that way? No. She thrust that idea right out of her head. She just didn't dare believe anything nice about him. He was the man who had cast Liz off to cope alone, and if he thought he could win Terri's heart by first softening her aunt's then he had another think coming!

She arrived back in the bedroom to find them both waiting for her, Terri wearing a pair of white shorts and a yellow T-shirt. Carlo stood behind the child, tall and proud, his hand possessive where it rested on the child's shoulder.

He lifted his gaze to Cass, then went perfectly still, his eyes travelling over her from the fresh crackling fall of her quickly drying hair and down her slender figure captured in pale blue cotton.

'You are very beautiful, Miss Marlow,' he murmured huskily.

Startled by the unexpected remark, Cass just stared at him, shy heat pouring into her cheeks. He watched it happen with a kind of fascination that further upset her senses, and her tongue cleaved itself to the suddenly parched roof of her mouth.

Then, thankfully, Terri was breaking the moment, her voice soft and dreamy. 'My mummy was the most beautiful lady in the whole wide world,' she sighed. 'Wasn't my mummy beautiful?' she enquired of her father.

'Yes,' he answered gruffly. 'She was very beautiful.'

Cass was instantly hostile again. Kill that if you dare! she defied him over the top of the child's head, and he had to look away, his tanned cheeks drawing inwards.

'Come on,' she said to Terri, holding out her hand to her. 'I thought you were hungry, and Mr Valenti won't bother to feed us if we don't get a move on.'

But Terri was too busy frowning over some small problem of her own to notice the hand. 'If he's my daddy,' she asked her aunt, 'then why do you call him Mr Valenti?'

The air was suddenly too thick to breathe.

That was the last thing Cass had expected her to say, and, by Carlo's reaction, the very last thing on earth he had expected to hear! He jerked to attention, his gaze blackening with enough emotion to completely overlay his composure. And Cass quivered as the steel bands around her chest tightened.

It was over. That first hurdle she had deliberately in-stigated with a resentment which cut deep into her soul was now negotiated.

She looked down at Terri's frowning little face, won-dering achingly how much confusion was tumbling around the little girl's head if Cass's own head was whirling with the complexity of it all! Then she caught the child's hand in hers and said, with as much cool as she could muster, 'Because he is Mr Valenti to me. But what you call him, Terri, is your own decision.' Then, with an outward calm that nowhere near reflected the turmoil clamouring inside her, she turned towards the suite door. 'Where do we go from here, Mr Valenti?' she enquired, and knew that he knew she was asking far more than just the way to the food Terri had demanded.

Carlo made for the door, his back ramrod stiff, and his face carefully averted from both of them as he led the way out of the suite. Cass and Terri followed hand in hand across the hall towards the door which opened on to the central courtyard. He didn't glance around, didn't show any sign that he was even aware they were there, and Cass's aching heart went out to the little girl, who was suddenly very subdued. She had made a monumental move towards him just then by announcing that she knew who he was. And Carlo, fool that he was, had not risen to the occasion.

Terri would not easily forgive him for that.

'Maria!' The woman was just crossing the courtyard as they appeared, and, hearing her name called, she stopped, turning that beaming smile on them as Terri let go of Cass's hand to run towards her.

'What the hell do you think you're playing at?' Carlo's hand, coming like a manacle around her wrist, spun Cass around to face him.

'What did you expect me to do?' she threw back angrily. 'Terri asked the question and I told her the truth! Did you expect me to lie?'

'You bitch!' he spat, his face so white that his eyes glowed black against the taut skin. 'You couldn't even give me a chance to coax her into liking me before you struck!'

'You ungrateful swine.' Cass gave a violent tug at her captured wrist. He refused to let it go. 'How long would you have kept the truth to yourself?' she demanded. 'I know how your twisted mind works, *signore*! You've already proved you don't care a damn about anybody's feelings but your own!'

'That is not true!' he denied. 'I——'

'You've been so busy compiling your dirty dossier of lies about my sister,' she cut in bitterly, not interested in anything he had to say, 'that you didn't even notice that you had a far more powerful weapon over me than your filthy slander of Liz!'

His head went back, hauteur blocking out his discomfort at her bitter attack. Cass flayed him with her eyes, a malevolence she had never known herself capable of holding her features tense and hard.

'It didn't once occur to you, did it, that if I was prepared to fight you to hell and back to protect her mother's memory then I wasn't about to disillusion her about her thankless father? God,' she choked, so angry that she was trembling with it, 'she's part of both of you, dammit!' Tears stung hotly at her eyes, the tremors running through her so violent that he had to feel them. 'I could no more hurt that child by poisoning her mind about you than I could cut her little throat! You only had to say to me that you were going to inform Terri of who you were, and you would have had me beaten! She likes what I like, loves where I love!' As the emotion began to take her over, so her voice deepened into a husky vibrancy. 'From the moment she set eyes on you she felt some kind of affinity. I noted it straight away. I thought you did too, but all you saw,' she derided contemptuously, 'was your own personal goals and what your cynical intelligence told you how to achieve them! Oh, get your hand off me!' she choked, tugging at her imprisoned wrist. 'Your touch makes my skin crawl!'

Carlo had stood so utterly silenced by her outburst that Cass would have found it funny if she weren't so angry. But her final cutting remark sent the air sucking into his lungs, and he snapped his hand away from her, his harsh face closing like a door being slammed tight shut.

'As you say, Miss Marlow,' he murmured stiffly, going all Italian on her by executing a curt bow. 'I seem to have misjudged you, and for that I apologise.'

'But not for the lies you've concocted about my sister.' She refused the apology, turning away from him in time to see Terri disappear through a door with Maria. 'Where you could only think of yourself and your wants,' she went on tightly, 'I can only consider Terri's. My own feelings dare not even be given air space—or you can be assured, *signore*, that she would be screaming blue murder now rather than skipping trustfully beside one of your damned servants!'

They glared at each other across the width of the open doorway. He looked ready to kill her, and she was angry enough to wish he would just try it! She had never felt so physically roused by another person before. It was as though every impassioned sense she possessed had ignited in response to this man.

And just look at him! she thought in angry resentment. His neatly styled black hair had hardly a strand out of place, when, metaphorically speaking, Cass had just dragged him by it to the ground! He wore his clothes as if they had been made exclusively for him—which, she then cynically supposed, they probably had! And the body beneath had a whipcord power to it that disturbed her whenever he so much as came near her!

He disturbed her in a lot of ways, she acknowledged as the silence between them stretched to breaking-point and still they continued to glare at each other. Just about every sense she possessed was on red alert, and throbbing in warning against him! Sexual aggression simply oozed from him. Angry or not, cold-hearted or not, the man had something which made her own stomach twist in response, and forced her to accept why her sister had been so captivated, so damned gullible with him!

She shuddered, blinking herself firmly out of her breathless trance—only to feel the heat sting along her cheeks when she caught his eyes intent on her. While she had been dissecting Carlo Valenti, he had been doing the same thing to her!

Their eyes met, and something deeply personal passed between them. Shaken by it, she went to turn away, but his hand came up, fingers curling around her chin and lifting it so that she had to continue looking at him. He didn't speak, those long fingers cool against her flushed skin, but something in the dense blackness of his gaze made her quiver, and she stood transfixed by it, wanting to deny it, scoff at it even, but knowing she couldn't.

The sound of skipping feet had them jerking apart, and Cass turned her head in time to see Terri come running back across the courtyard. The child stopped in front of them, her eyes flicking sharply from one taut adult face to the other.

'Maria says there's food through that door over there,' she informed them slowly. 'I came back to get you, Cass,' she said, in a way that told both adults whom she gave her allegiance to.

Carlo gave a small grimace, and Cass involuntarily matched it as she struggled to pull herself together.

'Really?' she answered over-brightly. 'Then let's get to it, kiddo—before you fade away!' And she reached out to take the little girl's hand.

It was only as they reached the door across the courtyard that Terri seemed to remember her father. She stopped, turned and frowned when she saw him still standing where they had left him, his thoughts turned entirely inwards.

'You can come too, if you like,' she invited off-handedly, and Cass had to smile at the child's guile as she coolly ordered the master of this beautiful place around as if he were a servant.

Thick black lashes lifted in time to catch that smile, his eyes darkening in a way which trapped the air in Cass's lungs and flicked at the fragile tenure of her control once again. Then he was coming towards them, his movements so lithe and graceful that both she and Terri watched him, unable to drag their eyes away.

When he reached them, his daughter gravely offered him her spare hand. Carlo smiled, and just as gravely accepted it. 'Thank you,' he said.

'You're welcome,' replied Terri in a way which set the fine hairs on Cass's body tingling. They had sounded so very alike then.

It was a strange trio who moved from the inner courtyard to an outer terrace, where the warm air was weighed down with the sweet scent of summer blooms. In front of them the wooded hills rose lush and green, the late afternoon sun sparkling just above the tops of the trees.

The terrace was shaded by a latticed canopy laden with heavily perfumed flowers. In the centre of the floor stood a round table set for four, and sitting at it was the most elegant old lady Cass had ever set eyes on.

Now what? she wondered.

CHAPTER FOUR

THE woman smiled as they approached. 'Ah, so you are here at last.' With a slow deliberation she rose to her feet, the silk of her dark blue dress rustling as she moved. 'Good afternoon, Miss Marlow,' she greeted politely, but her eyes were fixed greedily on Terri's curious face, the open desire to know and love so strong that even Cass could not suspect it.

'This is Signora Elicia Valenti, Miss Marlow,' Carlo formally introduced. 'My mother,' he explained, then went down on his haunches beside his daughter, and, by using her name quietly, demanded the child's attention. 'This nice lady is your *nonna*, Teresa, and she has been wanting to meet you for a very long time.'

Mrs Valenti started jerkily, the action almost over-balancing her from her precarious, half-standing stance, and the fingers she had been resting lightly on the table-top tensed, her lined face paling as she shot her son a concerned, questioning look. Carlo gazed steadily back, and silent messages passed between them.

His mother, Cass guessed, had not expected that instant reference to her relationship to Terri, and she was stunned by it.

'*Nonna?*' Terri repeated slowly. 'What's a *nonna*, Cass?' She gave a questioning tug at Cass's hand.

'A grandmother, poppet,' she explained. '*Nonna* is the Italian name for a grandmother.'

Her small brow puckered. 'I haven't had one of those before, have I?'

'No, darling, you haven't had a grandmother before.'

54

'Will I like having one?'

While the other two people present were essentially ignored by the child, Cass endeavoured to answer this rather awkward question. She began by joining Carlo at Terri's level while all around them the air began to buzz with a listening tension.

'Grandmothers, Terri, are specially made to love little children,' she gravely informed her uncertain charge. 'Some children are lucky enough to have two grand-mothers, while some have none at all, but you, darling, have this one, who looks very nice to me.'

Terri turned her frowning gaze on the poor subject under discussion. It was turning out to be a day of days for her, Cass noted ruefully. First she is kidnapped, then she wakes up in a strange room with an even stranger woman sitting beside her bed. Then she finds out she has a daddy, then a grandmother, when really she had been quite content without any!

'Are you nice?' the blunt child demanded of Mrs Valenti.

The old lady smiled, real amusement lightening her brown eyes. 'Oh, I do hope so,' she confided. 'I have certainly had no complaints so far from my other grandchildren.'

'You've got more than just me?' Terri took a hesitant step towards this brand new phenomenon.

'Three,' her grandmother announced. 'Two boys, and another little girl who looks just like you.'

Two more steps brought Terri beside the old lady's chair. 'Can I see her?'

'Thank you,' Carlo murmured under cover of Terri's voice, bringing Cass's head swinging around in his direction. Their faces were disconcertingly close. Close enough for her to see the fine black shards flecking the dark brown iris. He wasn't smiling, but his mouth was softer than she had seen it before, soft enough to draw her gaze down to it as he added quietly, 'It was more than—fair of you, in the circumstances.'

He had the most beautiful features, she was thinking hazily. His tanned skin smoothly stretched over the Roman shape of his bones. Everything about him was smooth, sleek, elegant, even the way the hairs grew in a subtle arch across his brows.

She was staring again, and flushed when she realised it. 'You're welcome,' she mumbled, mimicking Terri's trite remark of earlier. Then stood up quickly, her bright head tilted at a haughty angle which utterly denied that short but unnerving trip into intimacy. 'Who do the other children your mother mentioned belong to?' she asked him as he came up straight beside her.

'My sister, Louisa,' he said, sliding his hands into his trouser pockets. 'She lives with her husband in South America so my mother has few chances of seeing them... As you can see——' his glance slid over to where his mother was carefully lowering herself back into her chair while holding Terri's attention with her soft voice '—she is not strong. She had an accident some years ago which has left her severely weakened. From living a very busy and active social life, she is now content to spend her time here. I would prefer it,' he then added carefully, 'if our—battles were restricted to when she is not around to witness them.'

'Please, Miss Marlow, do sit down!' Mrs Valenti suddenly became aware of her manners, inviting Cass to take the seat to one side of her. 'And you, Teresa, will sit on the other side of me, please?'

The child obeyed, her fascination with this new being by far outstripping her until now unimpressed view of her father.

As if by tacit agreement on all sides, the light tea was enjoyed with a lessening in the hostility, both Cass and Carlo for the moment content to watch and listen to the easy way with which Mrs Valenti charmed her grand-daughter, holding her attention by asking her questions about herself and listening intently to the serious little replies she received.

'I have been upstaged, I think,' Carlo murmured drily as he offered to refill Cass's coffee-cup.

'By a past master at it, I should imagine,' she smiled, then was immediately serious again. This whole thing was slipping too quickly away from her own control. It had been one thing dealing with an undeserving father, but it was quite another having a real live grandmother to contend with also. *'Signore——'* she began carefully.

'Carlo, please,' he inserted. 'My mother will be offended by such formality from someone she considers family.'

'I am not family, *signore!*' Cass declared in a driven whisper. She flashed him a look. He was smiling lazily at her, refusing to be drawn by her anger. 'We are not even friends, come to that,' she added. 'We are on opposing sides of the fight, remember.'

'So we are.' Those dark Italian features looked almost satanic as he flashed her a wide white grin. Her heart missed a beat, this damned acute awareness she was experiencing of him another battle she was having to fight against. 'But for now we will call a truce, I think. For the *bambina's* sake. For my mother's sake. So sheath your sharp claws, Cassandra.' A tanned hand came out to cover her own. 'We will fight again later.'

He said the words as if they were a lover's promise, and Cass snatched her hand away, glaring at him as he came smoothly to his feet. 'If you have satisfied your hunger, Teresa——' he turned his attention on his daughter '—I have something to show you, if you would like to come with me?' Tentatively, he offered her his hand.

Terri didn't look too sure. 'What is it?' she demanded suspiciously, then, because she couldn't help it, 'Will I like it?'

'I acquired it especially for you,' he answered drily, 'so I do hope you will like it.'

It took a moment, but curiosity eventually won out over the reserve Terri was putting up against him. She scrambled down from her chair to join him, her hand slipping into his as they walked off together.

Cass watched them go, her attention locked on the battle of emotions going on inside her. One part of her wanted to run after them so that she could shield Terri from the man who had caused her mother so much pain, but the other, less bitter side of her nature could see the vulnerable desire to love and be loved in the way Terri gazed curiously up the length of her father's shape as she walked beside him.

They disappeared from view, and a sigh broke from Cass's lips as she turned back to the table.

A silence fell, with neither Mrs Valenti nor Cass seeming able to find anything light to say to each other. Cass took refuge in her cup of coffee, sipping at it while she pretended an intense interest in their surroundings.

'They look well together,' Mrs Valenti eventually broke the long silence.

'Yes,' Cass quietly agreed.

'I see nothing of her mother in Teresa's outward appearance.'

'No.' Cass's mouth went wry at the relief Mrs Valenti could not erase from her voice. 'My sister was a true platinum blonde with skin as fair as mine. Terri most definitely takes after her father in looks,' she added drily.

The older woman looked assessingly at her. 'Then you must also see, Miss Marlow,' she continued carefully, 'how criminal it was for your sister to have kept the child's existence a secret from my son?'

About them spread the remains of a pleasantly shared tea, enjoyed beneath the warmth of a sun shining golden in a pure azure sky. Cass glanced at Mrs Valenti, and saw with a sinking heart that her lined face had lost its warmth. She had been putting on an act for the benefit of the other two, but now it seemed the mask was off and in its place the kind of hard-eyed intention which set the tension buzzing between them.

'Maybe my sister was convinced that your son would not wish to know,' she suggested, knowing she could say more, but wouldn't. That was for Carlo Valenti and his guilty conscience to do.

Momentarily startled by the reply, Mrs Valenti then shook her head. 'No,' she denied, 'I cannot believe that. My son has always behaved with care and consideration towards others. If your sister led you to believe that Carlo would not wish to acknowledge his own child, then she lied,' she said firmly. 'If Carlo had been aware of her situation, then I can state—without question—that he would have done his duty towards both mother and child!'

'Well, I question it,' Cass retorted, green eyes flashing a look which Mrs Valenti's son had already begun to read as ominous. 'It's fine for you to sit there informing me of your version of the truth, knowing you have your son within easy calling distance to verify everything you say. But my sister is d-dead, Mrs Valenti.' Her voice broke on the word, and she swallowed thickly. 'Liz can't speak, can't lie, can't come back and defend herself against people like you who think they can sit in judgement on her when really they know nothing—nothing! But I'm still here,' she warned. 'And for as long as I can draw breath inside my body, I shall protect Terri from the likes of you and your son—and anyone else who would try to hurt her!'

'We have no wish to hurt the little one!' Mrs Valenti looked at Cass in horror, her old face gone white as a sheet.

'You hurt her every time you think badly of her mother!' Cass cried, coming angrily to her feet. 'What will happen if I leave Terri in your care, *signora*?' she challenged hotly. 'Every time she does or says something you don't quite like, will you blame it on her mother's influence? Will you deride Liz at every opportunity you get—deprive Terri of the God-given right to openly love her own mother?'

'No!' the older woman denied, taken aback by Cass's fierce attack.

'I see you've let the tiger loose, Mamma,' a grim voice drawled from the terrace doorway.

Cass swung around to find Carlo leaning against the open door-frame, tanned arms folded across his white-shirted chest. And her flashing eyes darkened with anxiety as she searched the space around him for Terri.

'She is with Maria—thank God,' he said grimly. 'For your voices could be clearly heard right across the valley!'

Sheer relief sent Cass sinking heavily back into her seat.

'I thought we agreed not to bring my mother into our—battles,' he reminded her curtly.

'You forgot to tell your mother the ground rules,' Cass muttered, shaken by her own carelessness. If Terri had overheard them. If she'd...

'I do believe, Mamma——' straightening, he came towards them '—that I did set certain—ground rules—for this meeting before I would allow it to take place. Here, drink this.' He handed Cass a fresh cup of coffee, and it was only as she took it from him that she realised just how badly she was shaking. 'And one of the most specific points I did insist upon——' he returned his attention to his stiff-faced mother '—was no derogatory remarks about the mother of my daughter!'

'She may be your daughter,' Cass inserted angrily, 'but she is still legally in my charge—and will remain so as long as you people persist in trying to bully me to get your own way!'

'Bullying or no,' Carlo inserted, 'I do, most succinctly, get your meaning at last, Miss Marlow. Which is not so surprising, I suppose, since you have been trying to hammer it home to me with a hatchet since we first collided with each other!'

'Well, I suppose that's something.' She sipped at the strong hot coffee in an effort to stem the angry tears she knew were glittering in her eyes.

'And in so being,' he continued, 'if you have finished biting every Valenti head off you can snap at, may I suggest that we adjourn to my study where once again we will attempt—and please do note the word *attempt*——' he made sardonically clear '—to find some compromise to this—mess—which will be agreeable to *all* of us?'

'Terri may need me,' Cass confessed, resenting his tone.

'Teresa——' he used the name pointedly '—is quite content helping Maria with her baking, and my mother will no doubt join them to help hold the child's attention while we—talk.'

A questioning glance at his mother brought the old lady struggling to her feet. But it was only as Cass saw her reach for her walking-sticks that she realised just how feeble her physical health was, and she instantly felt guilty as she watched her move laboriously away. 'I shouldn't have lost my temper with her,' she murmured contritely.

'No,' he agreed, 'you should not. But I do accept there was provocation. My mother, you see, protects her family as fiercely as you do your own.'

'Point taken,' Cass conceded.

'Good.' His fingers closed around her arm. Startled by the hot spark of electricity which shot between them, Cass flinched, almost upsetting the cup of coffee in her hand. 'That's what temper does for you,' he taunted softly as he drew her to her feet.

'Oh, shut up,' she muttered, pulling away from him, more troubled by her reaction to his touch than the taunt. Her arm was still tingling as she followed him into the house, the odd sensation spreading out to encompass the rest of her body.

In his study again, this time he invited her to sit in one of the deep leather armchairs set by his desk while he moved around to place himself in the chair behind.

Unlike the modern suite of rooms she and Terri had been allotted, the study was furnished on more traditional lines, with a deep red carpet covering the floor and the furniture old and fine enough to be antique.

'I think I can immediately put this meeting on the right footing by doing something about—this . . .' The manila file appeared on the top of the desk again. 'If I am willing to destroy this file and withdraw the—threats I made earlier, will you reconsider your refusal to discuss Teresa's future with me?'

Cass looked at the file, bit down hard on her bottom lip, and began to sift through quickly what he had said in search of the hidden catch. Whatever was inside the file—lies or not—she would do almost anything to see it gone.

'Destroying that file does not remove the fact that you actually compiled it,' she pointed out, 'and nor does it remove the fact that you were willing to pay my sister to rid yourself of any responsibility she had a right to expect from you.'

Something violent flashed in his eyes, irritation at her stubbornness, Cass suspected, feeling her pulses quicken as she held on to that look, demanding acknowledgement of that one point if nothing else. She was not about to pull her punches with him. She knew his sins, and he knew she knew. The file or not, Carlo Valenti was the one who had sinned against her family, and not the other way around.

His hard gaze shifted to the manila file, then he sighed almost defeatedly and said, 'I can, if you will allow me, explain my own side of all of this.'

Her bright head shook. 'Not if you're going to slander my sister again,' she said. 'Because I just refuse to listen.'

He smiled at that, a grim half-cut of a thing which lifted one corner of his attractive mouth. 'Damned if I do and damned if I don't, Miss Marlow?' he murmured drily.

'You see, Mr Valenti,' Cass quite seriously explained, 'there really can be no excuse for what you did, no matter what the circumstances.'

He got up, a touch of irritation in his movements as he spun to face the window behind him where his valley sat bathed in the warm orange glow of a slowly dying sunset.

A silence fell, the only sound in the room, the steady tick of the Venetian cased wall-clock hanging above the fireplace. Cass watched him clench and unclench his fist once or twice before he thrust it impatiently into his trouser pocket, and found herself chewing on her bottom lip, half wishing there was some way he could come out of this smelling cleaner. She was beginning to acquire a reluctant respect for this man who was prepared to go to such lengths to get his own way.

He turned suddenly, honing directly on to her sea-green watchful eyes. 'You are quite right, of course,' he conceded at last, a grim parody of a smile touching his eyes with a sombreness he made no effort to hide. 'There are no excuses worth voicing.'

He sat down again, shifting the file to one side in a way that said it now disgusted him as much as it did Cass. 'But I will say this,' he went on firmly, 'and without reserve. From the moment I discovered my daughter's existence, I have had only one aim in life, and that is to make up for the years she has been deprived of a father's love and support!'

'By threatening to take her away from me, who has loved and cared for her since the day she was born?' Cass challenged. 'By putting us through hell over the last twelve months while you pursued us like some avenging devil?'

He sighed in exasperation, then took a firm hold on his Latin temper. 'I concede that this whole thing between you and I began very badly and has proceeded to deteriorate ever since. Twelve months ago, when I made that phone call to you, I had only just learned that I had a daughter, and I was in a state of severe shock. I frightened you with my admittedly arrogant demands,' he acknowledged, 'and naturally you took flight before I had a chance to explain to you what my intentions were.'

'"To bring Terry back here to live with you",' she quoted his own words of twelve months ago right back at him.

'No!' he denied. 'I wanted to bring you *both* here to live!' he corrected, bringing her green eyes flicking up to his to see the grim sincerity written on his face. 'For the last twelve months, Miss Marlow, you have been running, and I have been chasing after you to tell you just that.'

A new silence fell, one where at last her resolve to fight him to the death began to waver.

'At no point over the last twelve months have I ever meant either you or Teresa any harm!' he insisted fiercely.

'Except for that file.' Cass eyed the offending manila file with distaste. 'That took a great deal of time to compile, going by its thickness. That, Mr Valenti, smacks very much at a desire to hurt, to me.'

'Forget the file,' he growled, finding its return into the discussion irritating—then caught Cass's dry expression, and grimaced. 'OK——' he sat back heavily in his seat '—so, desperate measures called for desperate means. I had come to the end of my patience with you, and the file was designed for the exact purpose I used it for—to pull you into line the moment I got close enough to use it. In the end it was my ruin,' he then ruefully conceded. 'You make your point, Miss Marlow, with the lethal thrust of a rapier! Now I wish to talk terms,' he continued briskly. 'I want to get to know my daughter, and I want her to have a chance to get to know me. And I also think that, in your heart, you believe we both deserve that chance.'

He was right of course. In all conscience she had no right to keep father from daughter or vice versa. But, in allowing that mammoth point, it left a very bleak picture of what was left for herself. And, selfish or not, the idea of losing Teresa frightened Cass enough to force her restlessly from the chair, her face pale as she turned away from him.

The room was long and wide, with windows at either end. Cass found herself pacing the thick red carpet covering the floor to the opposite end of the room. In marked contrast to the view behind where he sat, this window looked out on the central courtyard where the quickly dying sun could barely penetrate. She could just make out the Venetian pots spilling with bright summer blooms, and the fountain sprinkling out fresh, clean water into the dry summer air.

As she stood there staring bleakly out, she saw her niece appear, skipping backwards as she chatted ten to the dozen to the old lady who appeared with her, leaning heavily on her walking-sticks as she moved.

'They feel something for one another already,' Carlo's voice said quietly just behind her, and Cass sighed shakily, ready to burst into tears.

As they watched, his mother stopped walking, her silvered head bending to catch something Terri was saying to her, then the old woman's head went back and she laughed out merrily, the sound ringing off the heavily perfumed walls.

Carlo's hands jerked up to grasp Cass's shoulders, and his voice pulsed with some deeply felt emotion as he murmured thickly, 'She has not laughed like that for years—not since the car accident she was involved in took the lives of my wife and my son, and left her as you see her now.'

'Y-your son?' Cass turned in his grasp to stare at him in horror. Of the several sharp shocks she received from that roughly voiced statement, the fact that he'd once had a son shocked her the most. 'I'm so sorry...'

'He was just four years old when I—lost him,' he said, 'and as blonde as Teresa is dark...' The words died, lost inside his thickened throat. Cass looked at him in mute sympathy, the only feature she could distinguish in the glowing gloom his eyes, shot raw with a deep and personal pain.

'You still miss him.' Not a question, but a husky statement of fact. It was written all over the tensely held face.

The hands absently curving the rounded cups of her shoulders gripped tensely. 'We all miss him,' he said. 'He was a beautiful child.'

'And—your wife?' Almost against her will Cass found herself asking the question. They were standing very close together, the emotion of the moment linking them by a mutual experience of loss.

'As Teresa would no doubt say...' a smile of pure whimsy softened the tense lines around his mouth '...she was a princess. A beautiful golden princess...'

Cass stood, as stifled by his sadness as if it were her own, imagining that close and happy family who must have once lived in this valley in contentment. This man with his beautiful wife and son. That poor old lady out there who must have believed nothing could ruin their happiness. Then she thought of Liz and her disastrous relationship with Carlo, and suddenly she could not believe him capable of being as heartless as she had made him out to be. It just didn't fit with what she now knew of him. A man who had loved and lost one child did not casually discard the chance of loving another.

His gaze flickered down to collide with hers. They didn't speak, and, as they stood there gazing sombrely at each other, the dimness began to close them in, the silence, until it felt as if they stood alone in a dark, dark chasm of mutual sorrow, their bodies close, linked together by the sad mood of loss. A strange emotion began to stir inside Cass, the merest flicker of something alien to her budding into life and holding her attention focused on it in an attempt to identify just what it was. Then he moved, his dark head coming slowly downwards until his mouth met the full, soft quiver of her own.

It was nothing like the attack he had laid on her earlier. In fact, it was not like a kiss at all in the real physical sense, but more a spiritual search for something they had instinctively recognised in each other. She stood passive in his arms, her face turned up to the kiss.

'Cassandra,' he murmured, 'can we try to be—friends?'

'Friends.' That's what this is, she thought as his mouth came back on to her own again, a gesture of friendship between us, nothing more.

His lips began to move on hers, gentle, searching, as light as gossamer, and as beautiful as life itself. 'I'm sorry,' she heard him say, and wondered hazily what he was apologising for.

His hands still curved her shoulders, gently moulding the sun-kissed warmth of her skin left exposed by the thin-strapped style of her dress, fingertips lightly caressing until they met with the silken fall of her hair, where they closed, tangling themselves into the thick bright mass of fire, to tug, ever so gently, until her throat was arched and her mouth was fully presented to his. Her hands slid up to grasp his waist. His skin felt hot to the touch beneath a covering of fine white linen. She sighed softly, and so did he.

'You taste of roses.' Again, the remark was made within the boundaries of the passive embrace. No hint of threat, no sexual implication. Cass closed her eyes, and allowed a growing flood of warmth to permeate her senses.

She must have trembled because he muttered something in Italian, and drew her closer to him, fitting her into the muscled contours of his body, drawing the breath from her on a shaky sigh which parted her mouth and allowed the moist tip of his tongue to explore the trembling opening.

She felt the intimacy of that caress like a lick of fire, and suddenly she was clinging to him for dear life, as sensation, the like of which she had never known before, began to shimmer through her. He pressed her closer, moulding her to the long, hard length of his hot-skinned frame, and all at once the passivity fled, chased away by a hot tide of pleasure which thoroughly shook them both.

'*Dio!*' Carlo dragged his mouth away from hers. '*Dio*, forgive me, I did not mean to——!'

He jerked right away from her, breaking all body contact so that Cass stood there dazed and swaying, watching him through a haze of shocked sensuality, flinging himself to the centre of the room.

'Damn,' he muttered, then, 'Damn,' again.

She closed her pulsing mouth, her tongue flicking out to collect the moisture left there by his caressing tongue, and she heard his muffled choke as he spun his back on her. Then silence fell on the darkened room, consuming the air until it was almost impossible to breathe in it.

'Are you all right?' he asked after a while.

'Yes,' she breathed, feeling no more 'all right' than he sounded. It had shaken them both, that strange kiss which had felt as if their spirits had touched briefly.

'Will you think over what we have discussed?'

'Yes,' she breathed again, unable to conjure up another single solitary word.

'Then go now, and find Teresa. My mother will have taken her to your suite by now. It is time for her bed, I should think.'

'Ye——' It started to slur thickly from her tongue, but she managed to drag it back this time, watching through the crazy daze as he moved stiffly back behind his desk and abruptly sat down.

'Cassandra...' he sighed, and her name slid from his tongue like a caress, taking what little air she had left and trapping it in her lungs '...please leave here before I make a complete mess of everything and kiss you again—for real this time...'

'Oh!' The mere fact that she was just standing there staring at him like a love-dazed idiot brought her tumbling back to life.

'Yes—oh,' he mocked, but, even so, the mockery was half meant for himself, his smile wry as he watched her move hastily for the study door. 'And—Cassandra?' he stalled her as the door came open in her trembling hand.

'Yes?' she whispered anxiously.

'Believe me, I did not mean that to happen.'

'I know,' she mumbled, unable to look at him, and glad of the enveloping darkness which hid her girlish blushes from him. Neither had she. Yet it had happened, and the results were far more worrying than the reasons for the kiss. 'It—it was just the—influence of the moment,' she excused them both shakily.

'Something like that,' he agreed, and she heard rather than saw his rueful smile as she made good her escape.

CHAPTER FIVE

THE hectic flush was still high on Cassandra's cheeks when she entered her allotted suite. Beyond the half-open door to Terri's room a series of excited shrieks told their own story, the sound of Mrs Valenti's gentle voice and the more jolly one of Maria telling her that Terri was enjoying her new-found family.

Cass sighed shakily, her confusion mixed with a disturbing sense of personal uncertainty. What in heaven's name was happening to her?

'Ah, Cassandra!' Mrs Valenti appeared in the doorway to Terri's room, her smile a little uncertain. 'I hope we do not intrude, but Maria and I have been helping Teresa into her night-things.'

'And she's been leading you a merry dance in the process, I would hazard a guess.' Cass managed to make her voice sound light with effort.

'She is certainly a very lively child,' the older woman agreed, then added more seriously, 'I—I wish to apologise to you, my dear, for the—altercation we had earlier. Will you please forgive an old lady her rudeness so that we can be friends?' Leaning heavily on her sticks, Mrs Valenti sent her an uncertain smile.

Cass felt her heart go out to this woman who had lost so much in one brutal blow. 'Of course,' she said warmly, 'I——'

'Hey, Cass!' Thankfully, another voice cut through the awkwardness as Terri bounced into the room. 'Where've you been?'

'Talking to your daddy,' Cass informed her niece.

71

'Did he tell you about my present?'

'Present?' Cass blinked, having forgotten all about the present Carlo had taken his daughter off to see.

'Her name is Lucia,' she was told importantly.

'Whose name?' Cass frowned down at the child.

'My pony, of course!' Terri sighed impatiently. 'Didn't he tell you about her? She's got hair the same colour as yours, and a tail as white as cotton wool...'

A pony? Cass was thinking. Carlo has given Terri a pony? Anger began to rumble up inside her, thankfully dispelling all those other far more disturbing feelings she'd been struggling with. So, that was what he was up to, was it, using a different kind of blackmail?

Coercion to love!

'He said she's to be my very own, and that I've got to learn how to look after her properly, and how to ride her nicely, and he has a horse called Lucifer that looks the exactly same only he's bigger, and I've not to go near him 'cos he bites!'

'Who, your daddy?' Cass quizzed.

'No, silly,' the child giggled, sending a look of exasperation at her rapt audience, 'his horse!'

Daddy bites too, thought Cass drily, feeling the warm blush mount her cheeks all over again.

'I think it is time we allowed you to settle the little one down,' Mrs Valenti inserted ruefully, the look she sent her telling Cass that she was aware that Terri was becoming over-excited. 'Goodnight, Teresa dear.' Bending low on her sticks, she placed a kiss on the child's brow, her brown eyes darkening when Terri put up a small hand to touch her cheek. 'Dinner will be served in an hour, Cassandra,' she informed her huskily, her face averted so that they couldn't see how moved she was by Terri's little gesture. 'Maria will come and sit with the little one so you may eat with a peaceful mind.'

But Cass refused dinner that evening. With Terri safely asleep, she decided that she had a lot to think about, and there was no way she was going to set herself up for further confusion by having to endure another couple of hours of the Valenti unique brand of company.

A frown creased her smooth brow as she sat cross-legged in the centre of the luxurious bed. She was dressed once again in her own shorts and T-shirt, having put them back on the moment they were dry enough to wear. And that in itself had been an act of defiance, she admitted. As though she was making some kind of personal stand against events she had so quickly lost control of.

Five years of well-shored prejudices were beginning to tumble down in a matter of a few hours of being in the company of the man they had been so firmly erected against. It felt as though weeks had gone by since their eyes had first clashed outside Giuseppe's garage, instead of a mere half a day!

The few things she actually knew about Carlo Valenti were only what she had read in the articles written about him in the newspapers. And those had left her with a cynical picture of a man who lived, breathed and slept with his ego. Yet the man she had come to know a little today had shown her a completely different person.

Certainly, the ego was there. A man couldn't dress, look, speak and behave as he did without there being a generous dollop of egotism in his make-up. But she'd also seen compassion in him today, and a surprising depth of understanding—plus a real sense of fair play. He had actually backed down about that awful file of lies about Liz because he had come to accept how unfair he was being.

He'd had her beaten with that file because there was no way she could risk Terri hearing any of those lies about her mother. And she sensed he had known it. Yet remove the threat he had—or promised to do, which, with another frown, Cass found she trusted him to do.

Sure, he had a temper, she argued with herself, but so did she! And they did seem to spark each other off quite spectacularly.

But would he be a good father for Terri?

A picture, of a golden-haired little boy running into his father's waiting arms, shot like a pain across the forefront of her mind, followed quickly by a woman, as fair and lovely as Liz had been, smiling tenderly at the man she loved...

He must be attracted to women with blonde hair, she mused with a grimace at her own bright red tresses. That put her right out of the running.

Now, why had she thought that?

Because you are attracted to him, she answered, then dived off the bed to stand wide-eyed and trembling with shock at that telling confession.

One kiss and you're anybody's, she accused herself with a feeling of near hysteria that had her suddenly prowling relentlessly around the room. Perhaps that's your biggest problem, she decided bitterly. Not enough of those said kisses in your life to learn the art of indifference. You're just a push-over for a practised rake like Carlo Valenti! You've been too busy playing mother to bother with men, and now look where it's got you! Perhaps, she followed that thought through, it was time she did something about it!

And that kind of thinking was just asking for trouble, she told herself derisively, and it did nothing to solve the dilemma she was in about Terri.

Carlo was right, she allowed—Terri needed the reassuring strength of a father's love to support her through the growing years. She now had a grandmother to offer her the female support she would need. Here, in this place, she had all the opportunities the world could possibly offer her, waiting within a fingertip's reach.

Little Miss Cassandra Nobody could never begin to compete with that. And, if Carlo was determined to take a serious interest in his daughter's life, which, she conceded firmly for the first time, he was definitely going to, with or without Cass's approval, then her own importance in Terri's life would diminish steadily...

A long sigh shook her, and she folded her arms across her body in that age-old search for comfort. Maybe it was time to let go completely. Go back to England, leaving Terri where she knew she would be happy and safe. Maybe, she followed on, she hadn't been doing the child any favours at all by keeping her away from these people who so obviously wanted to love her...

A knock at the suite door brought her swinging around to frown at it. 'Come in,' she invited, irritated by the intrusion.

Carlo stepped quietly inside, putting her instantly on the defensive as a warm flow of embarrassment swept through her body.

'Maria tells me you have declined dinner,' he said, his expression strictly polite.

'Yes.' As an answer, its clipped tones verged on the rude, but Cass couldn't do much about it when the mere sight of him was enough to disturb her now. Her hooded gaze flicked restlessly over him. He was dressed semiformally, in black silk trousers and a pure white silk shirt that accentuated the richly tanned colour of his skin and did little to hide the cluster of dark hair she could see shadowing his rock-solid chest.

Her mouth went dry, and she spun away, wishing to God she'd never set eyes on him.

Her curt reply had made his face harden fractionally, and the way she turned her back on him brought a stiff silence clambering down upon their heads. Carlo seemed to be hesitating over something; she could sense his thoughts fixed broodingly on her, and tiny shivers began chasing themselves up and down her rigid spine.

'Is Teresa asleep?'

Cass nodded in mute reply. So that was it, she was thinking. He was here because he was concerned about his daughter, and not her own refusal to eat with them. For some reason that annoyed her even more, and, rudely keeping her back to him, she stared down at her bare feet curled into the cool creamy tiled floor.

Really, a less arrogant man would have taken the hint and left her alone with her black mood, but he didn't. Instead, and after another brief silence which had the fine hairs on the back of her neck tingling disturbingly, he stepped further into the room and quietly closed the door behind him.

'I realised, only a moment ago when Maria came to me, that I had not made it clear to you that you are no longer being held here under duress. You are free to leave whenever you want to, Cassandra,' he informed her deeply. 'Both you and Teresa,' he then made clear. 'Though I would consider it an honour if you would both accept the hospitality of my home for the remainder of your stay in Italy...'

Such a very gracious speech, delivered by a man who must pride himself on his good manners. But Cass had to force herself to respond, turning to face him with a cool smile.

'Thank you for saying it,' she acknowledged, 'but I had come to realise that.'

His slow nod accepted her generosity. 'Then why do you refuse to eat with us?'

'I'm—tired...' she invented weakly. Well, what else could she say? she thought in frustration as his sleek brows arched in wry disbelief. That I simply don't want to be anywhere near you? That you upset and confuse me just by being here? That I'm frightened of you and I think it's best that we steer well clear of each other because I am becoming dangerously attracted to you?

And you, Mr Valenti, have only one use for women like me.

Liz's image swam up to taunt her. The kind of woman Carlo Valenti went for. The kind of woman her sister must have been.

She spun away again, restless confusion in every line of her slender frame.

'My mother informs me that Teresa likes her room.'

'Who wouldn't?' she snapped, then realised just how badly she was behaving, and gave herself a mental shake. 'I'm sorry. There was no call for that.' Spinning around again, she grimaced in apology. 'But, as you can no doubt appreciate, I have a lot of things on my mind at the moment, *signore*, and I'm afraid I'm not good company tonight.'

He smiled at the *signore*, but made no remark on it. 'And I intrude,' he graciously understood. 'Please——' he offered her one of the formal bows he could use to such devastating effect '—forgive me. I will leave you to your—thinking.'

'No!' The word was out before she could stop it, and her heart clattered in her breast. But he was turning back to the door, and suddenly she didn't want him to leave!

Oh, God! she thought wretchedly, not understanding herself any more. It was a bit like being on a balance scale: one moment she was eager to see the back of him, the next, wanting him to stay. 'Y-you can go and see Terri for yourself if you would like to,' she offered awkwardly. 'Y-you won't disturb her once she's fast asleep...'

His dark gaze levelled thoughtfully on her for a moment, whatever he was thinking hidden behind the polite mask he was wearing tonight.

'Thank you,' he said at last, and warm colour flooded her cheeks again—why, she just didn't know!

With the smooth grace of a man who was in total control of his own body, he moved across the creamy floor to the connecting room where his daughter lay sleeping the enviable sleep of the innocent.

Cass followed slowly, unable to stop herself. She had a morbid desire to see that love he had claimed for Terri confirmed. It might be like hammering another nail in her own coffin, but she needed to do it anyway.

He was squatting down beside the bed, his harshly handsome profile thrown into stark relief against the soft glow of the small lamp left burning close by.

Terri was curled into her usual ball. The only thing showing among the mound of bright yellow was the thick silken mass of jet-black curls. Carlo put out a hand to gently stroke them, his expression so fiercely tender that Cass couldn't drag her eyes away from him.

'My son was very like his *mamma*,' she heard him murmur huskily. 'But this little one is so like me, it——' He swallowed, and there was a suspicion of a glitter in his eyes as he turned them on to Cass, and her heart squeezed in her breast in aching sympathy. 'There is something almost reverential in seeing oneself re-created in another human being——' his gaze slid back to his sleeping daughter '—like the achievements of one's karma. I am fulfilled.'

Cass felt unutterably moved by the words, by the rare compliment he was paying her by revealing such deep and personal feelings to her. 'Your wife must have felt the same sense of fulfilment when she looked at your son,' she offered softly.

He nodded, sending the sleeping child one last lingering glance before straightening to stride swiftly from the room. 'I will have Maria bring you a tray,' he informed her over his shoulder, his long stride taking him quickly to the suite door, 'and I wish you goodnight.'

'Goodnight, Signor Valenti,' Cass whispered to the closed door. He had already gone. Left so swiftly that she knew he'd had to get away before she witnessed his emotional breakdown.

That man, she found herself thinking positively, is no more capable of harming another human being than I am.

Which left her feeling even more confused. What had really gone on between him and Liz?

The next morning, Cass went in search of Carlo Valenti.

Maria had served them breakfast in their room, then taken Terri off to visit her grandmother who, apparently, did not leave her suite until noon.

Cass was back in her T-shirt and shorts, hair pulled into a simple pony-tail. Maria had waved her towards the terrace when she'd enquired where Carlo was, and, sure enough, she found him lounging over coffee and his newspaper, looking cool and relaxed in a cream short-sleeved shirt and buff-coloured riding breeches.

He stood up as she approached, his expression smiling but guarded. 'You slept well?' he enquired, moving swiftly to hold a chair for her to sit down.

'Yes, thank you.' She hadn't, but it seemed churlish to say so. In fact, she'd had an awful night, battling with herself. 'I want to talk to you,' she told him bluntly. Having reached some firm conclusions around dawn this morning, she was now determined to tell him what they were before she changed her mind.

Dark eyes sharpened on her, his long hands pausing in their folding of his paper. Without asking her, he poured some coffee into a clean cup and pushed it across the table towards her.

'I am due back in England in just over a week.' His nod told her that he was already in possession of that information—how, she didn't know, and couldn't be bothered going into right now. The man had his ways; she already knew that from experience. 'I would like to use those days left to see how Terri responds to you. And...' she took in a deep breath before going on, because this next part was going to be difficult to say '...and if, during that time, I can feel reasonably sure that she is prepared to accept your presence in her life, then we will talk terms, as you call it—try to come up with a solution which will suit all of us, but mostly Terri.' Her slender shoulders lifted and fell, sun-kissed and shining in the early morning sunlight. 'I am prepared to bow to whatever Terri decides she wants——' even if that means my leaving her here with you, she added bleakly to herself '—so long as you are prepared to do the same.'

'Her welfare is of paramount importance to you, isn't it?'

'Of course!' she declared, ruffled by his dry tone. 'Do you think I have taken care of her all this time out of some morbid sense of duty? She's my sister's child, please remember! My blood runs in her veins just as your own does! I love her, and of course her welfare is paramount!'

'I was actually referring—badly, I admit——' he smiled a little at her display of temper '—to the fact that you put her needs way above your own. Don't you ever wonder what your life would have been like without the responsibility of a small child to dominate it?'

'No.' Her soft mouth firmed. Until I was brought here, I never had the time to bother considering myself, she thought heavily. Things were so much simpler that way! 'I am a trained nanny by profession. The only difference Terri has made to my life is that I have been caring for a child who is related to me rather than some other family's child.'

'Without the weekly wage-packet to make it all worthwhile,' Carlo inserted quietly.

'How did you know that?' Cass gasped, shocked that he should know that Liz had paid her no wage in the real sense of the word.

'You forget, I have made it a—hobby of mine to find out everything I could about you and your lifestyle.' His gaze narrowed on her. 'One week,' he said, swinging them back on to the real issue under discussion. 'You do not give me long to prove my worth to my daughter. I cannot see how I can meet such a short deadline...' A new self-mocking smile touched his attractive mouth. 'You know as well as I do that she does not like me very much.'

'She doesn't dislike you,' Cass felt urged to point out. 'She's just—reserving judgement on you for now, that's all. I should be able to tell within the week which way she is going to go.'

Both brows rose enquiringly. 'And what special powers do you possess which will enable you to make such a rapid judgement?'

'Nothing so sinister as witchcraft, if that's what you're thinking,' she laughed, the amusement actually reaching the deep sea-green of her eyes. 'I will simply wait to hear her call you "Daddy"—or not, as the case may be. At the moment, she refers to you as "he", "him", "that man", or any other version on the same theme she can come up with which gives you no real title at all. She hasn't forgiven you yet, you see, for not responding to her reference to your parentage yesterday.'

'I was taken by surprise,' Carlo defended himself, faint traces of colour spreading across his strong cheekbones. 'The last thing I had expected you to do at that time was inform Terri of who I actually was.'

' 'Rule number one in the nanny's book of wise advice, Mr Valenti, is never tell a child an outright lie.' Cass sent him a small smile. 'Children have this nasty little habit of catching you out. And rule number two,' she went on with soft emphasis as she got up to leave him, 'is don't try buying their affection. They'll only hold you in contempt for it, if you do.'

'I must assume that remark is in direct reference to the pony?'

Cass nodded curtly. She was still angry about the pony.

'The pony was not so much a bribe,' he defended, all at once adopting his high hauteur, 'but what I saw as a good way to bring Teresa and myself together for long enough periods of time for us to get to know each other without other adult influences getting in the way. I intend to teach her to ride myself,' he informed her stiffly. 'An hour or so every day in the low pasture with just myself and Lucia, her pony. I am hoping that, while she is learning to trust my guidance as a tutor, she will also learn to trust me as a father. I don't believe in leaving things to time and fate. Teresa needs me, and the sooner she realises that then the sooner we can begin to build a more healthy relationship.'

'And I apologise for misjudging you,' Cass bowed to that stiffly offered explanation. 'If it helps redeem me a little,' she added as she turned to go, 'Terri would speak of nothing else this morning but your promise to show her how to ride.'

His smiling nod accepted Cass's olive-branch. 'And what will you do with yourself this morning?'

'Oh . . .' Cass let her gaze wander over the lovely valley '. . . I'm going to explore, I think—unless you have your henchmen lurking out there primed to shoot me on sight!'

Carlo laughed, coming smoothly to his feet. 'You will be quite safe to go where you please during your stay here,' he assured her. 'But I was thinking...' he went on, coming to join her as she moved across the terrace towards the house '...as I have to go into San Remo this afternoon on business, you may like to come with me so you can collect your things from Giuseppe's?'

'Thank you,' Cass said, relieved, because she had been wondering how she was going to get there without having to be a nuisance to anyone. 'I'd like that.' The sun caught at her shining hair as she swung her face up to smile at him. Carlo watched the fascinating effect of fire on fire as Cass went on thoughtfully, 'Terri will probably take a nap this afternoon—would Maria watch over her, do you think?'

Dark eyes took a moment to flicker into focus on hers. 'I think Maria would be delighted,' he assured her. Then made her start in nervous surprise by reaching up with a hand to touch her hair. 'You are very, very lovely, Cassandra Marlow,' he murmured huskily. 'Both inside and out.' Then he turned abruptly away, leaving her standing there feeling—she didn't know what she was feeling, except more bewildered, more confused.

She took one of the pathways which led into the hills behind the house, clambering higher and higher through the rows of fruit terraces which made the valley a profitable concern as well as a private haven for the Valenti family.

Breathless and hot with climbing, she came upon a small clearing which gave her an uninterrupted view of the valley below her. The narrow river was glinting prettily in the sunlight, the white-painted house standing out against its lush green surroundings.

It was a beautiful place, idyllic in its dramatic setting. And Cass took a deep gulp of fresh, clean air. It was good to be alone for a while. She was given the opportunity so rarely these days. Taking care of a lively five-year-old could take its toll on the most rugged spirit!

She leaned back against the thick trunk of an old olive tree, sheltering from the sun beneath its gnarled branches while she rested. It was then that she caught sight of a bright flash of colour in the pasture below. It was a yellow T-shirt dancing along beside a tall, unnervingly familiar man. He was leading a small pony by the reins, his other hand locked firmly with the child's, while she, by the way her dark head was bobbing, was talking her usual ten to the dozen.

Cass watched Carlo tether the pony to the fence, then bend to lift Terri into his arms, holding her close as he reached out to stroke the pony's snowy white mane. He was trying to encourage Terri to do the same thing, but she was more intent on studying his face at such close quarters. Cass could read every thought and expression flitting through her niece's mind, even from this distance. And her heart squeezed in aching understanding. The poor darling wanted so much to reach out and stroke him rather than the pony, learn the feel of his skin, its clean, smooth firmness.

Her own hand twitched, remembering, and she felt herself go pale. Everything was becoming so complicatedly interlinked within her mind that she was finding it difficult to distinguish her natural concern for Terri from a concern on her own behalf! It was as if the pair of them were treading a parallel line—Terri in learning how to accept Carlo's love as her father, and Cass learning how to accept him as a man she could quite easily fall in love with.

It was frightening, worrying, very, very disturbing. He was in danger of becoming an obsession. Even now, from so far away, she could feel an inner vibration which seemed to flow from him into her and back again.

As if he too picked up the vibrations, his dark head lifted suddenly, eyes lancing up the hillside to where she stood. He couldn't possibly see her standing here beneath the shade of the olive tree, she was sure of it. He didn't have the advantage of height to help him, and the sun had to be in his eyes. But she felt the fierce burn of his gaze as if he had actually reached up and touched her, and she quivered, the feeling leaving her shaken and perplexed.

CHAPTER SIX

LUNCH was a relaxed affair—mainly because Carlo didn't join them. 'Busy catching up on business in his study,' his mother explained as they gathered on the terrace.

Cass had changed into another of the provided sundresses in a soft lilac print that set off the bright glow of her hair. And, although she felt uncomfortable wearing clothes she hadn't bought and paid for herself, she was aware she looked good—fit to be seen out with Carlo Valenti, at any rate.

They had finished lunch and were listening to Terri giving them a blow by blow account of her first riding lesson when the sound of high heels tapping on the tiled floor brought all three heads swinging around to watch the open doorway.

Sabrina Reducci appeared, looking as if she'd just stepped out of the centre-fold of *Vogue*.

'Ah, Sabrina!' Carlo's mother welcomed warmly. 'This is a pleasant surprise!'

'*Buon giorno, Zia Elicia.*' Sabrina laid her smooth cheek against Mrs Valenti's. 'I came here to see you yesterday, but that naughty Carlo sent me away!' Her lush mouth pouted sulkily.

'He told me,' the older woman confessed. 'He will be here soon, so I will make him apologise to you, Sabrina. But for now, you have met our very special guests, I believe?'

'Ah, yes, briefly—though Carlo did not seem to think it worthy of a formal introduction.' Her expression said she was still piqued over Carlo's rude dismissal of her the day before.

'Then let me do so properly now,' Mrs Valenti offered. 'This is Miss Cassandra Marlow,' she began, turning her warm smile on Cass. 'Cassandra, this is la Signorina Sabrina Reducci—a friend of our family from the time she ran around this valley in pigtails with my daughter Louisa, their only ambition in life to tease and torment poor Carlo.'

'Now I torment him in other more—subtle ways,' Sabrina smiled suggestively—a smile that died away completely as she turned to look at Cass. 'Miss Marlow,' she acknowledged coolly, offering the kind of aloof nod of her sleek dark head that Cass suspected she would use to someone she considered not quite the thing.

'Miss Reducci,' Cass nodded back, keeping her own tone strictly polite. After all, she thought wryly, she was quite prepared to admit that she was not in Sabrina Reducci's league.

'And this,' Mrs Valenti continued proudly, 'is my granddaughter Teresa!'

'Terri,' the child automatically corrected, her gaze fixed curiously on this new, elegant being who had come into her small sphere. 'You dress like my mummy did,' she told Sabrina. 'She used to wear nice dresses like that, and smell nice like you, only her hair was the colour of sunshine, and she smiled with her eyes.'

Out of the mouths of babes, Cass thought ruefully, as she watched the startled movement Sabrina gave at the unexpected shrewdness of the child's final observation. She didn't much like it, either, going by the way her mouth tightened, Cass noted.

But Sabrina recovered quickly, sending Terri a more relaxed smile as she lowered herself into the chair beside her. 'But you are very like your papa, no?' she quizzed lightly. 'You have his brown eyes and silky black hair...'

And his blunt manner, Cass added silently, on a wry smile to herself.

'You are enjoying living here, Teresa?' Sabrina asked.

Instantly, the child's face closed up. 'It's all right,' she mumbled, refusing to pass judgement on anything here yet—except perhaps her pony, and maybe Maria because they didn't understand each other and that amused her.

The lukewarm reply took the smile from Sabrina's lips, and sent her almond eyes in search of a new quarry, which, of course, had to be Cass. 'And how long are you hoping to stay here, Miss Marlow?' she enquired.

Cass frowned, not sure she liked the tone Sabrina had used—or the inflexion she had placed into certain key words in the remark. Nor was this a subject she wished to discuss in front of her niece, and the cool expression she lifted to Sabrina told the other woman so.

'It all depends,' she answered non-committally. 'At the moment, we are enjoying the Valenti hospitality too much to want to think about returning home.'

'Ah,' Sabrina nodded sagely. 'I understand your reticence, Miss Marlow. You will find it a wrench to leave Teresa behind here when you go.'

Terri's face came out of her glass, ears pricked and buzzing on that potentially explosive remark. Cass's green eyes began to spark ominously. And Mrs Valenti jumped in quickly before Sabrina really put her foot in it. 'Don't be so meddlesome, Sabrina!' she scolded, glancing pensively from Terri's frowning face to Cass's angry one. 'Or I shall have to tell my son how you try to make trouble.'

'Doesn't she always?' a deep voice drawled, and Carlo himself came into view, looking absolutely devastating in slate-grey trousers and a pale blue shirt. 'What are you up to now, you aggravating witch?' he grinned at Sabrina and bent to kiss her on both cheeks.

'I won't stay here with you when Cass goes home,' his daughter informed him promptly.

Carlo went still, all his good humour leaving him. Slowly he turned to face his daughter, and Cass caught Sabrina's small grimace as she too turned to study Terri's defiant little face.

'I do not remember inviting you to, Teresa,' he answered coolly. The child glowered at him, any hint of the companionship they had built up during their riding lesson gone in a flash. *'Grazie, Sabrina,'* he muttered *sotto voce*.

'I meant no malice, Carlo!' Reaching out, she laid a coaxing hand on his bare forearm where the dark hair grew thick and crisp, red-tipped fingernails curling firmly muscled flesh. 'I just did not realise that——'

'Your lack of perception has always been your worst fault, *caro*,' Carlo drily inserted before Sabrina could pour more oil on the troubled waters.

'Oh, you're going to be horrible to me again!' she cried, pouting in a way that was both sulky and provocative. 'You threw me out of here yesterday, and now you are scolding me for something I did not understand!' She sat back in her chair. 'When I think about it, Carlo, you are quite the rudest man I have ever met, and if it weren't for Zia Elicia——' she sent Carlo's mother a warm smile '—I would never set foot in this valley again!'

'Then I apologise for my rudeness and beg your humble forgiveness,' Carlo drily conceded. 'For the idea of you never coming near here again fills me with horror!'

He was being very false and terribly mocking, but Sabrina took it all as if he had gone the whole hog and gone down on his knees in front of her, and preened herself like an exotic bird.

'Teresa...' Carlo returned his attention to his still glowering daughter '...Maria has come to take you for your afternoon nap.'

'I'm not tired,' she told him, then spoiled it by yawning widely. 'And anyway,' she added stubbornly, 'Cass will be lonely without me.'

'I shall promise to take great care that your aunt does not pine too much without your company,' her father assured her. 'But Maria is looking forward to having you all to herself,' he appealed to the child's soft heart. 'Just look at her; she will be disappointed if you turn her away.'

Maria was standing by the open doorway, her round face expectant, and Terri looked at her from under lowered brows. 'Cass let me play in that great big bath in our room yesterday,' she recalled slyly, seeing herself in possession of a little bargaining power here.

Amusement sprang back into life in Carlo's brown eyes as he turned them on Cass. 'I see no reason why Maria shouldn't let you do the same,' he allowed.

Mollified, Terri scrambled down from her chair and was carried off by a gaily laughing Maria, while Sabrina Reducci was looking decidedly sour. 'You are going out, Carlo?' she demanded.

'To San Remo,' he explained, reaching down to brush his mother's cheek with his lips. 'So do not overtire my mother with your mindless gossip while I am not here to curb you,' he told her with a quick brush of his lips to Sabrina's cheek. He came to stand by Cass's side. 'Ready to go, Miss Marlow?' he enquired smoothly.

Cass stood up, relieved to have an excuse to get away.

'*Ciao*, then,' he called lightly, and took Cass's arm, leading her away with the red-hot needles of Sabrina's gaze stinging into her back as they went.

Were they lovers? Cass frowned thoughtfully as she walked beside him, finding that she was altering her opinion on that score. No man, surely, treated his mistress as cavalierly as Carlo treated Sabrina.

But then, she added cynically to herself, the way he had treated Liz had been worse. So maybe he could kiss and dismiss any lover without a qualm.

'Now,' he said, turning to look down at her as he guided her out into the sunshine. Cass's chin came up, the cynicism clear in her green eyes as they clashed with his. Taken aback by it, he halted, turning fully to face her. 'What have I done now?' he asked in genuine bewilderment.

'Nothing,' she said, and looked quickly away, frowning over her own confusion. Last night she had decided that he couldn't possibly have treated Liz as badly as she'd always believed him to have done. Now, after witnessing one short example of his behaviour towards Sabrina, she was condemning him all over again.

'Then why the accusing look?' he demanded, taking hold of her by the shoulders and drawing her closer to him so that she had no choice but to look into his questioning eyes.

Instantly she was aware of masculine hardness, his superior height and strength and potent sexuality. 'Y-you shouldn't treat her as casually as that, you know!' she blurted out.

'Who?' he frowned. 'Teresa?'

'No!' Cass shifted restlessly under his light grip. 'Miss Reducci! It isn't right. Not when she so obviously worships the very ground you walk on!'

He laughed, the sound nothing but a soft rumble in his cavernous chest. And the fingers cupping her shoulders tensed slightly. 'Sabrina and I understand each other very well, Cassandra,' he dismissed. 'Don't let our manner towards each other bother you so.' He moved back to her side, one arm sliding round her shoulders.

'I have to visit my hotel in San Remo for a while, but first we will attend to your belongings.'

He handed her into the car and closed the door. By the time he had stepped around the long bonnet and got in beside her, Cass was chewing thoughtfully on her bottom lip.

'Y-you don't have to wait with me while I pack my things,' she began awkwardly, not wanting to put him to too much trouble. 'If you can just drop me off at——'

'You must stop doing that,' he interrupted, bringing her head around to stare at him in puzzlement.

'Doing what?' she asked. She hadn't been aware of doing anything other than just sitting here!

'Pressing those neat white teeth of yours into that poor bottom lip.' If the words hadn't surprised the breath out of her body, then what he did next certainly managed it as he reached up to rub his thumb across the tender flesh of her bottom lip, urging the imprints left by her teeth to fade away. 'That's better,' he murmured, smiling when her lips quivered on a sudden influx of warm red blood. Then he turned and started the car while she just sat there, with her feelings towards him so complex that she couldn't say a word.

She was still floundering in her own confusion when he said moments later, 'You enjoyed your walk this morning?'

'Yes, thank you,' she answered primly, turning to look at him. 'I found a path at the back of the house which led up the hill...' The sun was shining down on them through the open sun-roof, filling that handsome face with such an air of strength and vitality that she stumbled over her words, and she had to look away from him before going on. 'Y-you live in a very beautiful place, *signore*,' she finished huskily.

'Yes, don't I, *signorina*?' he softly mocked, smiling at the faint blush that mounted her cheeks. 'We are very lucky in this part of Italy,' he went on more seriously, 'to be sheltered from the worst of the winter by the Apennine mountain range just behind us. The trees growing on the slopes are mainly good quality cedar, and there are some eucalyptus——' he flashed her another grin at her surprised expression '—they are not entirely exclusive to the Australian continent, you know. But closer to the valley bottom,' he went on informatively, 'we grow fruit: olive, lemon, fig, orange...' Another flashing glance at her made her heart flip unnervingly. 'No respectable Italian landowner would be without the fruits of the earth growing on his land! They are the symbols of our very culture—the humble beginnings from which we all sprang.'

'You've never had a humble thought in your life,' Cass derided.

Broad shoulders shrugged in lazy agreement. 'I count my blessing every day, Cassandra, be sure of it,' he said, not in the least offended by her sarcasm. 'San Remo itself, though hectic in the summer season, is a beautiful city, with its own unique brand of old-fashioned quality. And the road which connects it with Imperia further along the coast boasts some of the most spectacular coastline views in the world. Though,' he added, 'in my—admittedly biased—opinion, there are few views which can compete with—this...'

As he had been talking, they had been driving up through the trees on the other side of the valley. Now he brought the car to a stop on the crown of the hill, and turned to face her. 'What do you think?' he prompted.

Captivated, Cass let the air leave her lungs on a long and silky sigh. Out before them lay the rich royal blue of the Mediterranean, the sun glinting down on it from its azure heaven while Sam Remo lay far, far below them, basking in the benevolence of its relentless heat. Around the wide-sweeping bay, the chalk-white cliffs shimmered in a haze of silver heat, their sun-bleached walls topped by the road which ran precariously along its very edge.

'You were too preoccupied to take note of this on our way here yesterday,' he explained his reason for stopping.

'It's beautiful,' she breathed.

'Yes...' And something in the way he said that brought her head jerking around to find him looking at her, not the view. The breath stilled in her lungs, the mood inside the car suddenly tense and stinging.

'The colour of this dress suits you,' he remarked, touching a light finger to the curve of the bodice where it met the satin slope of her breast. 'I am—pleased to see you have made use of the clothes I provided for you.'

'A m-matter of necessity,' she said, willing herself not to jerk away from the burning sensation of his touch, trying desperately to keep her voice light, and wishing she knew how to deal with a man of his sophistication. 'It was either wear this or walk barefooted behind you while you pretended I wasn't with you at all!' she laughed a little shakily.

'Dressed in sack-cloth you would still be beautiful, Cassandra,' he said quietly, and there was no mockery whatsoever in his eyes.

'I...' She dragged her eyes away from him, so acutely aware of him and the sexual messages he was sending her that she could barely breathe. 'C-can we see your hotel from here?' Desperately she changed the subject, pretending to search the San Remo skyline for the distinctive shape of the Valenti Grande.

He didn't answer immediately, and the silence sparked in the air all around them, holding Cass stiff and unbreathing, her staring eyes seeing nothing but a red-hot haze of panic as he sat there watching her with those lazy fringed eyes and the kind of burning expression that set her blood racing in her veins.

The light brush of his lips against her shoulder sent all attempts to remain casual flying as she shrugged him shakily away.

'Stop it!' she choked. 'Please—please stop it!' Green eyes pleaded wretchedly with sensual brown. He didn't move, didn't speak, but the look in his eyes told her that, far from wanting to stop, he wanted to do more, much, much more. She drew in a shaky breath, the action lifting his fingertips where they still rested on the soft slope of her breast, and she shivered on the wave of sensual awareness that washed right through her.

What was it with this man, she wondered hectically, that he could manage to offset her with just the lightest caress? Had he used the same tactics to captivate her sister? Liz had been made up of much harder stuff than Cass. If she couldn't fight him off, then what chance did she have?

Already she was having to do battle with herself to quell the desire to just throw all caution to the winds and melt towards the pulsing sensuality of his inviting mouth.

This could not be allowed to happen, she told herself desperately. It would not be fair to Terri. It would not be fair to her sister's memory.

'For goodness' sake!' she whispered tensely. 'Don't make things more complicated than they already are!'

Her near panic must have got through to Carlo, because, after studying her strained face for a moment longer, he sighed and turned away. And Cass visibly wilted with relief as, without a word, he started the car again.

He drove them into San Remo, manoeuvring the car through the busy street with all the hot-blooded impatience of his race, jerking to a halt more than once just so that he could sound his horn at some poor unsuspecting tourist who wasn't used to dodging cars with the same dexterity as the natives. And, as she sat quietly beside him, Cass knew that more than half of his intolerance was due to the crazy atmosphere buzzing between the two of them.

It was sheer relief to see Giuseppe's garage come into sight, and she turned impulsively to Carlo. 'If you want to go and see to your business while I——'

'I will wait,' he clipped, dousing the engine the moment they came to a stop and climbing out of the car, his body movements so graceful that Cass had to wet her suddenly dry lips.

She got out of the car before he had a chance to come around and help her, so glad to see Giuseppe ambling towards them that she sent him a brilliant smile. It shocked the garage owner enough to make him grin appreciatively back.

'Go start your packing,' Carlo growled.

One glance at his frowning face and she decided not to argue, and walked off, feeling like a naughty child who had been sent to her room by her elder. As she mounted the cracked concrete stairs to her upstairs apartment, she could hear Carlo speaking to Giuseppe in crisp, terse Italian.

Giving out his orders, she suspected mulishly. Something he's very good at!

She had almost finished packing her one suitcase when he arrived through the open door. 'I have settled your account with Giuseppe,' he informed her. 'So when you are——'

'You've *what*?' Cass gasped, spinning around to face him, and suddenly back to being the fierce-eyed woman he had almost crushed with his damned sex appeal.

He was standing there like some lordly dictator, his expression revealing all his distaste of their Spartan surroundings, but he actually looked startled by her sudden attack on him. 'I meant no offence, Cassandra,' he said, his long hands spreading in a conciliatory manner. 'I simply thought it would be quicker if I paid the bill while you——'

'But I paid my dues here before I even stepped on to the plane in England!' she snapped, remembering how lucky she had been to get that late vacancy with the small package company she had booked and paid her holiday with. 'The cheating old devil!' she accused Giuseppe, green eyes beginning to flash. 'Well, we'll just have to see about this!' And with a glowering intention which held Carlo rooted to the spot in the middle of the small apartment, she stalked angrily out.

Five minutes later and she was back, her mood still angry. She found Carlo standing by the open balcony window. 'Here.' Reaching for one of his hands, she stuffed a wad of paper *lire* into it. 'I can't stand swindlers!' she muttered.

Carlo was looking at her as if she were a brand new species he had just discovered. 'You gave him hell, didn't you?' he murmured ruefully. He had overheard everything from the open window.

'He thinks that just because you're rolling in it he can cheat you out of your money without conscience,' she snapped, still seething. 'Well, I just put him right on a few basic rules of life, that's all. And you, *signore*——' she turned her anger on him next, firm breasts heaving, cheeks flushed and eyes flashing '—would do better asking before you go around sorting out other people's lives for them!'

'I do beg your pardon, *signorina*.' He sent her a mocking bow with a mocking smile to match his mocking humour. Then, with a sudden dry ruefulness, he said, 'I cannot remember anyone ever fighting my battles for me before. Thank you. I found it rather—refreshing...'

'Yes, well...' Calming down at last, Cass turned away from him. 'As I said, I can't stand cheats.'

'You are a strange woman,' he murmured quietly.

'No, I'm not,' she denied. 'I'm simply more respectful of what I have than you are.' She spun back to look him in the eye. 'You may have more money than you know what to do with, but, if you can't be bothered to look after what you already have, then you'll soon find yourself with nothing at all!'

The money still lay in a crumpled heap in his outstretched hand. His dark eyes were alight with humour, and he was having some difficulty keeping the amusement from his lips. Cass felt her cheeks begin to warm all over again, and wondered crazily why she had actually bothered when all he could do was mock her for her trouble. Then suddenly the ridiculousness of the situation got to her also, and her slow smile acknowledged it.

'He thought I was going to strangle him,' she laughed. 'He was frightened to death.'

'I know the feeling,' Carlo drawled, studying her in a way that set her pulses throbbing all over again.

Flustered, she walked out on to the small balcony, suddenly in desperate need of some fresh air.

The silence between them stung at her ears. She might be inexperienced where men of Carlo Valenti's calibre were concerned, but she wasn't a fool. Each time he looked at her the messages he was sending were becoming more obvious, less easy to deny.

She heard him move, and crossed her arms protectively across her breasts.

'A Spartan room,' he said quietly from just behind her, 'but with a priceless view. It is no wonder you linger, *il dolce campionessa...*'

'W-what does that mean?' she demanded warily, sensing a nasty taunt.

His laugh was low and husky, setting off warning signals all over Cass's trembling body as his breath warmed the back of her neck. 'It means—my sweet champion, nothing even vaguely offensive.' Then, calmly, with his body almost but not quite touching her own, he stretched a hand out over her shoulder and began pointing out recognisable landmarks.

It was just for show, an excuse for what was really happening between them, the tingling sense of awareness growing to an acute sharpness, aided and abetted by her burst of temper, followed quickly by their mutual humour. She could sense him actually having to fight the urge to touch her, and she had to fight her own desire to lean back into that hard-packed frame standing so close behind her.

'You see the yacht, anchored furthest out into the bay?' The long pointing finger directed her where to look. 'She is called *Amante di Mare*—Mistress of the Sea.'

Cass's eyes flickered into dim focus on the gleaming white yacht rocking gently on its anchor. It was easily the largest and most luxurious one in the bay.

'Yours?' she guessed, sounding husky-voiced. Every sense she possessed was honed exclusively on him.

'*Si,*' he confirmed. 'I use her to take me from resort to resort as a more—favourable way of visiting my hotels. And also for—*divertimento*...' his English was deteriorating for some reason, and Cass found it difficult to breathe suddenly '...a place to entertain my more important clients. One day,' he went on deeply, 'one day I will take you cruising with me, *caro*, and we will sail right around the coast from here to Nice, or maybe Monte Carlo...'

The gap between their bodies was diminishing with each word he spoke until the heat of his skin burned her through the thin cotton of her dress, and Cass closed her eyes, her breathing unsteady, dreadfully aware that she was in danger of becoming completely beguiled by this man. Her every sense was throbbing to the husky pitch of his voice, the soft brush of his breath against her cheek, his height and width and undeniable machismo...

'And in the evening...' At last he touched her, his hands coming to gently mould her shoulders, and Cass jumped as if she'd been stung. 'Easy, *amore*,' he murmured soothingly, and completely closed that gap between them so that she was trapped between him and the balcony wall.

'Please!' The plea escaped her on a husky groan as she twisted around with the intention of pushing him away from her.

'Please, what?' His dark eyes lowered to watch the way her hands trembled against his broad chest. 'You know what is happening between us, Cassandra,' he sighed impatiently. 'We are violently attracted to one another, so stop trying to fight it, for it only adds to the agonising frustration.'

'No!' She tried to push him away, arching her back in an effort to avoid the slow lowering of his mouth. He looked fierce and hungry, suddenly frighteningly eager. 'No, I don't want this!'

And she didn't! she told herself hectically. It was just the madness of the moment, and the difficult situation between them that was making them super-sensitive to each other!

His hands moved to her back, sliding down her slender body until they met at her arching waist, where her muscles felt as tensely stretched as piano wire. He murmured something deep in his throat, then pressed her closer, bringing a shocked gasp from her trembling lips when she recognised just what was happening to him.

'I have to kiss you,' he muttered, and, with her still trying to pull away from him, brought his mouth down on to hers with a kind of fiercely gentle passion that took her skimming back through the hours to that other kiss in the darkness when they had responded to each other with something completely detached from the physical.

Whatever it was, it had her melting against him, an arm going up and around his neck to hold on for dear life while senses she was only just beginning to realise she possessed heightened into full, ardent life.

'You feel it too!' he murmured triumphantly as he dragged his lips from hers.

'Yes,' she admitted on a shaken whisper. She felt it too; it was no use trying to deny it any longer. His body pulsed against her own, and she could barely think through the whirl of feeling tumbling inside her. 'But I don't want to!' she added on a choked little cry.

'I know,' he sighed, and took her mouth again with a kiss so devastating that her knees buckled beneath her, and Carlo had to tighten his grip to maintain his mastery over the kiss.

Above them the sun burned down upon their heads, and below them San Remo sat shimmering in her after-noon siesta. Nothing seemed to move but the hectic throb of their hearts where they pressed against each other.

'Giuseppe,' she gasped out thickly, remembering the garage owner's habit of taking his siesta in the shade of his scrappy old awning. He had to be able to overhear everything!

Carlo growled something deep in his throat, then caught her up in his arms to take her into the apartment.

The cool feel of cotton against her burning skin was the moment she realised that he had laid her down on the bed and was coming to lie beside her.

'No.' She put up a struggle in a last ditch attempt to salvage herself from what was threatening to take place between them.

'Open your eyes, and tell me you don't want this,' he challenged, taking her face in his hands and forcing her to look at him. 'Tell me that to my face, Cassandra, and I vow I will never touch you again!'

Oh, he was so clever! she thought wretchedly as she stared into the passion-hardened planes of his lean, dark face. Unlike her, he was no novice to this kind of thing. He knew she wanted him, he knew exactly what was happening inside her pathetically struggling body, and the mere idea of him never touching her again was enough to send her still.

Her eyes closed, copper-tipped lids fluttering down as her fingers went snaking up the heaving tautness of his chest, and her lids opened in helpless invitation to the sensual beauty of his mouth.

Her surrender brought a lusty growl from his throat. Then the words began pouring from his practised tongue—soft, gruff, seductive sounds in a language tailor-made for love. He kissed her brow, her closed eyes, her small straight nose. His lips brushed lightly across her cheeks to her temples, then down her jawline to the corner of her quivering mouth. And all the time he played this exquisite game with her senses, his beautiful voice swirled around them, shrouding her in such a haze of pleasure that she didn't even notice that his hands had drawn the bodice of the sundress down until she felt his hands close around the silken swell of her breasts, and she whimpered as his thumbs found and began to tease the pale pink buds.

'You like that?' he murmured encouragingly. 'You like to feel my touch upon your naked skin? Skin like silk and as warm as honey. You have a beautiful body, *mi amore*,' he continued his seduction with his voice, 'made for loving—made for *my* loving!'

His mouth came down on hers again, staking claim just as his words and hands had done, and she moaned under his passionate onslaught, moving restlessly beneath him, her fingers clinging to his hair, running in agitation down to his shoulders, then scraping in excited agitation down his spine.

'Remove my shirt,' he commanded against her mouth, and her fingers automatically went to obey, fumbling with the buttons, eager, fretful, desperate to feel and touch him as he was touching her.

The shirt came open, and she tugged it from the waistband of his trousers, sighing as he came right over her, pressing her down into the old mattress so that the bed-springs creaked under their weight. And she didn't care, didn't care if Giuseppe could hear them and would know what they were doing, because her hands were suddenly in touch with sleek, tight skin, feeling the hard ripple of muscle, the deep shudders of pleasure her touch incited in him. His chest heaved, the mat of crisp black hair rasping against her breasts. His mouth was fixed on hers, moving her lips to his own command, his tongue warm and moist and seductive.

The kiss went on and on, their caresses becoming more urgent, more sure as they were dragged down deeper and deeper into a maelstrom of pleasure until, on an impatient growl, Carlo stripped the dress from her body then lay half across her, so that his hands could explore the newly exposed curves of her body.

He was on fire, the sleek, taut contours of his darkly tanned skin burning against her palms. Heat lay in two dark streaks across his cheekbones, his long nose flaring with the effort it took him to drag in air to his lungs. His mouth was parted, and trembling slightly, lips pulsing with the inflow of warm, sensual blood.

And the words kept on flowing between hot bursts of passionate kissing, reducing Cass to a quivering mass of pure exquisite feeling, until she was crying out with every caress he laid on her.

'Touch me,' he urged, the plea roughened with passion as he took her hand and placed it against the taut flatness of his stomach. As the warm muscles beneath her hand contracted in pleasurable response, he captured the throbbing tip of her breast with his lips, drawing it deep into his mouth, his tongue rasping hungrily over the pulsing nipple, making her arch in wild response.

Oh, God, she thought crazily, as new feelings began tumbling one on top of the other, I shouldn't be doing this! This man is Terri's father. The man who had deserted her sister. The man who——!

On a cry that was almost driven, she wrenched herself free, pushing him aside to roll off the bed and stand, swaying, staring in a kind of dazed horror at the place where she had just been lying, beneath his suddenly still frame.

'Liz,' she whispered; that was all—just 'Liz', in that awful pained way, and all hint of passion drained away from them both.

CHAPTER SEVEN

CARLO got up, his dark face averted from her. Shaking badly, Cass bent to retrieve her dress, pulling it back on with icy fingers.

He moved back to the window, his fingers slow as they straightened his own clothing, and, in a silence so heavy that it throbbed between them, Cass went back to her packing, forcing herself to move about the room, checking drawers, the tiny bathroom, placing everything neatly into her suitcase.

When she had finished, she snapped the case shut, and sat down on the bed, too drained to even find the energy to tell him she was ready to leave.

'I won't apologise this time,' he said without turning to look at her.

'I don't expect you to.' She was all too aware that they had both lost control. Sex was a new and bewildering phenomenon to her; she hadn't realised it could take such a violent hold on everything sensible.

He was leaning against the open framework, staring out at the bay, a hand lost in his trouser pocket while the other picked absently at the peeling white paint. Cass felt her heart make a swooping dive, and knew it did it for him. He was a man, and a passionate one at that. She was uncomfortably aware that she had left it too late to draw back. Men weren't used to that—not men of his kind, anyway.

'Why do you have to be back in England by next week?'

The question took her by surprise. It was the last thing she had expected him to say next. 'I...' shaking her head, she tried to gather her scattered senses together '... I start a new job at the beginning of the new school term,' she told him huskily.

'Which is—when exactly?'

'The second Monday in September.'

'Just under three weeks,' he murmured thoughtfully.

'But first I have to find Terri and I somewhere to live, and...' Her voice trailed off, her teeth pressing down on her bottom lip when she realised just what she had said. Even she was beginning to accept that there was every chance she would be leaving Italy without her niece.

He turned to look at her at last, his expression under careful control. 'If I promise not to...' It was his turn to pause over his words, his mouth flickering slightly in a kind of self-meant contempt, then he sighed and began again. 'I cannot deny that I want you, Cassandra. I cannot even promise—as I was about to do—not to touch you again. Because if circumstances place us in a situation similar to this one...' A slow shrug completed what he wanted to say. 'But if I give you my word that I will— try to control my amorous instincts...'

She had to smile at his way of putting it, and so did he, which helped ease some of the tension out of the space between them.

'Would you consider staying on at my home until your September deadline?' he suggested. 'One week is really not long enough for me to get to know anyone,' he quite fairly pointed out. 'And I have contacts in England who could perhaps, with your approval of course,' he added quickly, being very careful not to offend her in any way, 'find the necessary accommodation for you. And I could perhaps show you some of the popular tourist spots on the Riviera, make this a real holiday—for all of us, perhaps, since I am not a man who takes time off from his work very often...'

Cass didn't answer immediately, having to fight a private battle with herself. The extra weeks in this man's company could prove disastrous to her own feelings. In the meantime it would also take Terri further and further away from her. But he was right—a week really wasn't time enough to give him a fair chance with his daughter.

'A holiday, Cassandra, nothing more,' he pressed her gruffly. 'Time to relax in the sun, and enjoy my hospitality, can only be good for both of you...'

'All right,' she agreed reluctantly, wondering even as she said it whether she was making the worst decision of her life. She was very much afraid that when those weeks were up she would be leaving Italy with nothing. Not Terri. Not even her heart.

The Hotel Valenti Grande was as luxurious as Cass had expected it to be. Carlo guided her across the forecourt from where he had parked the car, and, with an impersonal hand on her arm, he guided her behind the reception desk and into an elegant office, where he formally introduced her to his manager as, 'Miss Marlow, a guest in my home.' Nothing more, nothing less. 'Guido Renaldi, my manager,' he completed the introduction.

Cass saw the glint of interest light the younger man's eyes. 'Would that we all could have guests as beautiful, Miss Marlow,' he smilingly complimented her, and earned himself a scowl from his employer.

'I shall be as brief as I can,' Carlo said coolly, then strode over to the desk, placing himself in the chair behind it and snatching up the telephone receiver, his business manner as surely in place as his overriding passion had been earlier.

With all the inherent charm of his Italian nature, Guido Renaldi invited her to sit on the long cream leather sofa set along one wall, and joined her there. Then, either ignoring or just simply careless of his employer's narrow-eyed glare as Carlo sat barking out instructions via the telephone, he settled himself down to flirt outrageously with Cass.

She took it all in her stride, enjoying his amusing banter because it meant so little to her. Guido Renaldi had no chance of turning her head when it had already been turned by a past master at the art! she acknowledged ruefully.

When Carlo eventually came off the phone, his mouth was set and grim. 'How heavily is the yacht committed during the next three weeks?' he asked the younger man curtly.

Guido's dark brown eyes gave a flicker of amusement at his tone, but he answered smoothly enough, 'I don't know. I'll have to check. Why?' he then asked innocently. 'Who do you wish to impress with it—is it for business or pleasure you require it?' he then added goadingly.

It was obvious that Guido did not hold Carlo in any awe by his tone alone, but even he stopped grinning when Carlo said, 'Pleasure,' while sliding his gaze over Cass in a way which brought the colour pouring into her cheeks.

Cass shot to her feet, infuriated by the inflexion he had deliberately placed into all of that. Her eyes shifted to the amused face of Guido, and glinted calculatingly. 'Perhaps you would like to join us, Guido,' she suggested silkily, sending the manager a bewitching smile. 'We could make it a foursome—since Carlo will have his time taken up with Teresa. After all,' she added, 'it is for her sake that he wants to take the cruise...'

Sparks flew across the room while a hugely entertained Guido observed it all, reading into what she had said everything he was expected to read.

'*Grazie, signorina,*' he bowed graciously. 'I would be honoured to be your—companion for the day.'

'You may change your mind when I tell you that Sabrina Reducci is coming too.' Carlo's eyes held Cass's in cruel triumph as his counter-punch hit her firmly on the chin.

'Ah, no, Carlo, my friend——' Guido stared at him in horror '—not the lovely Sabrina also? You take two beautiful women for a day cruise on your yacht, and invite the very possessive Sabrina along?' He affected a disappointed sigh. 'I worry about you, Carlo, I really do...' Then he looked tragically at Cass. 'The man has no finesse!' he complained.

'I know,' she agreed, hating Carlo more than she'd ever hated him.

'Tell me,' Guido went on interestedly, 'what is this Teresa like? Will she be able to fight Sabrina for her handsome host's attention?'

Cass glanced defiantly at Carlo while he glared grimly back at her. The phone began to ring on the desk, and, still smiling, Guido lifted the receiver, then smiled even more when, after a moment, he offered the receiver to Carlo. 'It is for you, *amico*,' he murmured softly. 'Sabrina.'

The receiver changed hands, Cass and Carlo still locked in a battle with their eyes across the width of the room. 'Ah, *mi amore*...' he murmured, his deep voice dropping into the same huskily intimate Italian tones he had used with such devastating effect on her earlier.

Cass spun away so that he wouldn't see the angry self-disgust in her eyes. It all came so damned easily to him!

Guido moved over to her side, and gently took her arm. 'We will leave the *signore* to his—privacy, *signorina*,' he suggested quietly, 'while you and I adjourn to the restaurant for some refreshment.'

Outside the door, he burst out laughing. 'What is going on between you and my old friend?' he demanded. 'I have never seen him so uptight about a woman before— and a red-haired villain of a one, too!'

His dark head shook in rueful disbelief, and Cass turned a fulminating look on him. 'All that flirting with me in there was done just to tease him, wasn't it?' she accused.

'He deserved it,' Guido grinned. 'No man of Carlo Valenti's sophistication should wear his feelings on his sleeve and not expect to be teased about it! He could not take his eyes off you! Come,' he appealed to her with a disarming smile when her cheeks burned up all over again, 'forgive me for using you as bait. And allow me to take you for some refreshment to make amends.' His hand guided her across the foyer and through the doors of the restaurant. 'And you can tell me all about this mysterious Teresa, so I can then understand why you use her as a shield against the undeniable battle going on between you and my employer!'

But Cass had no intention of discussing Terri with Guido. If Carlo wanted to keep his daughter a secret, then it wasn't her place to speak.

'Aha!' Guido cried, when she didn't even smile. 'I sense a real mystery here.'

'Your English is very good,' she observed, deftly changing the subject.

He looked affronted as he held her chair for her. 'Of course it is good!' he exclaimed arrogantly. 'I work for Carlo Valenti! Nobody works for the Valenti organisation unless they are the best!' He took the seat opposite her, a smooth lift of his hand instantly catching a hovering waiter's attention. 'I speak fluent English, French, Spanish and German—besides my own native tongue of course. And can also get by in several Arabic dialects, and hold my own quite well in Japanese.'

'I do beg your pardon,' Cass laughed. 'And I speak only one language,' she admitted ruefully. 'English—very badly.'

'You do nothing badly, *mi amore*,' a deep voice drawled from just behind her, and Cass shivered involuntarily as two hands came possessively on her shoulders. '*Grazie*, Guido, for taking care of Cassandra for me, but...' Carlo was already propelling her out of the chair while his friend looked on in amusement '...we really don't have time today to linger and chat.' The last word was said as a clipped-off rebuke which seemed to sail right over Guido's elegant head. 'We will see you again soon, no doubt.'

'And with your other friend—Teresa—perhaps?' Guido taunted.

'Ah, yes...' Carlo paused in the process of turning away, his hands sliding down Cass's arm to take tight hold of her slender wrist '...my daughter,' he announced, and had the satisfaction of seeing the smile wiped off Guido's stunned face. 'Cassandra and Teresa will be staying with me for some time. Time enough for you to meet Teresa, I am sure. You will like her, Guido,' he smoothly assured his employee. 'She looks exactly like me—but she has Cassandra's smile.'

'Do you realise what you've just done?' Cass choked as soon as they were alone in the car with the dark head of Guido visible from the hotel doorway, his expression still stunned.

'*Mi scusi?*' he questioned innocently. '*Zi Eengleesh eet eez nota gooda!*'

'Your English is better than mine—and you know it!' she snapped, sitting stiffly on the edge of the Ferrari's cream leather seat, so angry that she couldn't relax back. 'You've just deliberately and intentionally made him believe that Teresa is our child! Which automatically implies that you and me have been...' She couldn't say it;

it dried up her throat to even try! She gave a short huff of disgust.

'Do not "deliberate" and "intentional" mean the same thing, *caro*?' Carlo murmured thoughtfully, slipping the car into gear and moving smoothly away. 'You are right, you know; your English is not good. Guido was asking for it,' he then inserted grimly. 'And so were you, flirting with him like that.'

'I can flirt with whom I please!' she informed him crossly, sending him a sparkling look. 'Just because you've decided that you wa——' Her lips snapped shut, horrified by what she had been about to blurt out.

But Carlo bore no such sensitivity. 'Want you?' he finished for her, watching her with scant regard to the road they were moving along. 'But we have established that fact already. And I made you an assurance that I shall do my best to keep. But don't think,' he warned, 'that I will also stand by and watch another man move in on something I am denying myself!'

'I belong to nobody,' she breathed, feeling a little desperate inside.

'You belong to me!' he ground out, sending the car flying as his foot went angrily down on the accelerator. 'As long as you stay in my home and care for my daughter, you, Cassandra Marlow, belong—to—me!'

'Do those rules cover your behaviour with the lovely Sabrina?' she couldn't resist sniping, revealing enough in that telling little remark to bring his lazy smile back.

'Any time you wish to put Sabrina in her place about me, then please be my guest,' he granted. 'I think I may even enjoy watching you do it.'

'Well, don't hold your breath,' she muttered.

The car swerved to a lurching halt, forcing other vehicles following behind them to swerve on a screech of burning rubber around them. Cass stiffened warily in her seat, eyes flicking nervously to the man beside her, who was in the process of lurching his lean body around so that he could glare at her.

'You always have to have the last word, don't you?' he ground out angrily. 'Always have to make the final thrust with your clever tongue before you can feel comfortable again!'

'Who said I was comfortable?' she choked, as aware of the chaos their argument was causing outside the car as she was of the chaos inside it. 'It's you who seems to have forgotten that I am only here because of Teresa!' she flared. 'Otherwise you wouldn't be giving me the time of the damned day!'

'You are here because we are crazy about each other!' he bit out roughly, the air rattling from between his clenched white teeth. 'And Teresa had nothing whatsoever to do with it!'

Cass looked away, knowing she was turning away from the terrifying truth in his words.

Slowly, the anger died from his eyes as he continued to study her flushed, confused profile, then he sighed heavily. 'Be calm, Cassandra,' he murmured drily, relaxing back into his seat. 'I have no desire to alienate you when we have only just begun to understand each other. These next three weeks were offered as a way for us all to get to know each other better, and that...' the car began moving again '...is what I intend to do with them.'

And that had been a firm decree, and not just mere hearsay, Cass discovered as he put himself out to turn their stay into a glorious whirl of doing together and being together. Each morning she and Terri were awoken to a new and exciting plan for the day.

They visited the old town of La Pigna, more affectionately known as San Remo's casbah, where Carlo led them through a positive maze of thin winding alleyways, up steeply climbing staircases and under narrow archways into dark, dark tunnels, where Cass clung tightly to his hand and Terri talked in high-pitched whispers of awe. Then, on a complete change of mood, he took them up Monte Bignone, smiling at their delighted gasps as the *funivia*—the cable-car—took them higher and higher to the kind of views that held them breathless. He showed them the weird ghost town of Bussana Vecchia and the fascinating prehistoric caves of Balzi Rossi, where the oldest findings of Neanderthal man had been discovered, the strange drawings etched into the cave walls flinging you back forty thousand years to a time beyond normal comprehension.

And when Cass thought she would overdose on too much history, he took them off to the beach, where she would find herself overdosing on too much tightly muscled, darkly tanned flesh when he stripped off without a care and got down to the simple pleasures of building sand-castles with his daughter or lazing in the shade of one of the big sun umbrellas, or running headlong into the sea when the inactivity got too much for him and he needed to swim off his excess energy. Or they would spend the day exploring his valley, following the river along its winding track towards the eye-of-the-needle gorge which guided the waters into the sea. Or tracking off along one of the dozens of pathways which led into the hills between terraces of sweet-smelling fruit trees and richly scented pines.

He held back on nothing, committing all their daylight hours to learning to know both of them, drawing Terri closer and closer to him with that magical mixture of gentle patience, firm handling, and such an open desire to love that the child could not mistake his sincerity—and using much less subtle means to keep Cassandra's awareness of him always on a low boil.

Not that he'd tried to seduce her again. But really that did not mean much. He still desired her, and his eyes only had to clash with hers to cause that stinging sense of awareness to leap between them, creating a sexual tension which was sometimes so strong that it transmitted itself to those around them. Terri was clearly puzzled by it, Mrs Valenti knowingly thoughtful, and Sabrina, beautiful, possessive Sabrina, who managed to get herself invited along on several of their excursions, grew more hostile towards Cass as each day went by. She demanded so much of Carlo's attention with her seductive manner towards him that, in turn, it made Cass feel vicious because it was so obvious by the way the man accepted all this adoration as his due that he considered it quite normal to flirt with several women at once!

Carlo Valenti was used to sophisticated women, women who knew how to play the game according to its sophisticated rules. Sabrina Reducci was one of those women, and, she forced herself to add, so had been her sister. Carlo had to know that Cass was not one of that worldly breed. So what was his ultimate motive?

He wanted his daughter, she answered herself. And if it meant seducing the aunt to get the child, then perhaps he was capable of being that ruthless. His treatment of Liz confirmed he could be, and the way he had pursued them over the last year said he could be relentless when set on achieving his goal.

And there it was, she concluded heavily during one of her long soul-searching exercises, the reason why she just didn't dare let herself fall into the magical web he was so cleverly weaving about them both: Carlo's motives just could not be trusted.

One week slid busily by, then the next. But, while Cass was finding it harder and harder to hold herself aloof from Carlo's sexual allure, Terri's defences remained strongly erected against him. Oh, she wanted to give in. Everyone who watched her with him had to be aware of it. They only had to see the long, wistful looks she sent him when she thought he wasn't looking, or note the way she was constantly finding excuses to touch him, to be close to him, to realise that she was really quite desperate to love him openly.

Cass understood what the poor child was going through because she was suffering from the selfsame struggles herself. But, whereas Cass had good and valid reasons for fighting Carlo's charm, on the face of it, Terri did not.

Yet still she held back.

'Aw, Cass, come on; you're dragging too far behind!'

Cass sent her niece a glowering look, then took a tighter grip on the reins as the big beast beneath her swayed too precariously for her peace of mind. 'I think this is a stupid way of getting about,' she complained, turning the glower on the man who was sitting so elegantly astride his own fabulous horse, cruelly laughing at her discomfort.

'You will get used to it, Cassandra.' Turning his mount, he trotted back to her side, his horse lightly picking its way over the loose stones by the side of the river. 'It is because you are having to use muscles you have rarely used before.'

'Tell me something I don't know.' Carefully she lifted one well-rubbed thigh away from the horse's flank. 'Did we have to come this far on my first real ride?'

Unlike with Terri, who had taken to horse-riding like a duck to water, it had taken Carlo more than a week to coax a very wary Cass into the saddle. She was a city girl, born and bred, and horses were alien beings as far as she was concerned.

'Another week, and you will be riding as though born to it, *mia caro*,' Carlo said soothingly as he came alongside her.

Another week, Cass thought bleakly, and I won't be here.

She gave a small sigh, her bright head turning wistfully up to the sun. She had come to love this place. Its warmth, its beauty, and its alluring tranquillity.

'You are tired.' Misreading the sigh, his amusement changed to an immediate concern. Carlo reached across the gap between them to cover her hands with one of his own, his dark gaze fixed solicitously on her.

'Yes,' she admitted, refusing to look at him—as always when he was close, much too physically aware of him. 'I think it may be better if I lead my horse back on foot while you and Teresa—— '

'No.' The hand holding hers moved, long fingers taking the reins from her so that he could lead her over to where Teresa waited impatiently. 'Here, mia cuore,' he said to his daughter. 'Take your aunt's reins for me while I——' he passed the reins to Terri '—bring her up to sit with me!'

'What are you doing?' Cass cried out as suddenly she found herself plucked from her saddle as though she weighed no more than his daughter, and dumped efficiently across his lap.

'I am making you more comfortable, caro,' he murmured suavely. 'Now, sit still so we can finish this journey the romantic way.'

'Romantic?' she snorted, refusing to let her senses respond to the high, tensile ripple of his muscled thighs. 'I see nothing even vaguely romantic in every bone in my body aching!'

'Mi amore, this is the most romantic encounter you and I have had in many days.'

'Weeks,' she corrected without thinking, then caught her lower lip between her teeth as the colour spread along her cheeks. If she hadn't been so dauntingly aware of the height she was now seated at on his big horse, she would have been leaping right off again, just to escape from that very telling stupid remark!

'Why can't Cass sit with me?' a petulant voice piped up.

Carlo glanced down at his daughter's disapproving face. 'Because your little pony will not take Cassandra's added weight,' he explained, 'and because we have been thoughtless enough to expect too much of her too soon. So now I make amends by pampering her a little, *si*?' he requested his daughter's approval, and received it with a dubious nod of her curly black head, and a pout that said she was still not happy with the situation.

She was jealous, of course, which was just another facet of the emotional struggle she was having with herself. She might not be ready to claim Carlo as her father, but neither did she like anyone else to get too close to him.

'Now, Teresa,' he instructed the child, 'you will have to lead the way back while I bring up the rear with Cassandra's mount. Can you manage that, do you think?'

Diverted by this bit of responsibility she was being given, Teresa tossed her head and prompted Lucia into movement. 'Of course I can,' she stated scornfully. 'You just take care of my aunt Cass!'

'Aunt Cass—Aunt Cass,' he mocked the child wearily as she moved away, her little body swaying to the pony's ambling gait. 'She is forever displaying her protective love of her precious aunt Cass! But when will she show the same regard for her papa?' His sigh was short and heavy. 'My mother and even Maria receive that same open display of love. It seems that she is prepared to love anyone so long as it is not me!'

'You know as well as I do that she virtually worships the very ground you walk upon!' Cass refused to offer him any sympathy. 'It really is only a matter of time before her defences come tumbling down.'

'Time is something which is quickly running out for me,' Carlo pointed out. 'No, Cassandra,' he sighed, as he prompted the horse into movement, 'it is obvious that she is never going to commit herself to me while she believes I hold only a temporary place in her life. We have to talk about it,' he decided grimly. 'Come to some decision about what we are going to do.'

Cass sighed, accepting that he was probably right, and a serious talk was inevitable, but she felt intensely reluctant to begin it, knowing that, once they did start talking, the halcyon world she had been existing in recently was going to topple down around her.

'But not today,' Carlo said briskly, as if he too was reluctant to spoil the easy rapport they had built up over the last two weeks. 'Tomorrow I take you on our promised cruise. The day after that should be soon enough to come down to earth.'

Happy to go along with that, Cass let her body relax into his. He smelled of fresh, clean air, the pale green shirt he was wearing open at the throat all the way down to the cluster of crisp dark hair at his chest, and she rested her head into the hollow of his shoulder, sighing the small sigh of the contented as his lips came down to brush her temple.

'Just think,' he murmured after a while, 'with Guido joining us for the cruise, you will be able to pay me back for all that flirting I have done with Sabrina over this last fortnight. I only hope,' he intoned pensively, 'that I will be able to control the urge to throw him overboard, as you have controlled the urge to scratch Sabrina's eyes out each time she's been here.'

'I have nothing against Sabrina!' Cass denied, not willing to admit to being that jealous, not for all the tea in China! This man was conceited enough as it was without her adding to it. 'I like Sabrina. It's just that she seems to have taken an immediate dislike to me.'

'Liar,' he drawled. 'You hate seeing her hanging on my arm all the time, monopolising me, kissing me...'

'You Italians throw your kisses around like raindrops,' Cass casually dismissed that one.

'And Sabrina certainly knows how to kiss a man,' he inserted teasingly.

'Have you no discretion?' Cass turned to glare up at him. 'Kisses for hello, kisses for goodbye—kisses in between for any excuse you can think of!' She affected a disapproving sigh. 'It's a wonder you know real passion when it hits you—or perhaps you don't,' she then decided. 'You Italians are known for your caprice, falling in and out of love at the drop of a hat.'

'Love is for the lovers, *caro*,' he chanted lightly, 'kisses are for friends.'

'I don't see the difference.'

'You don't?' His black brows arched in mock amazement. 'Then perhaps this will help you to understand.'

There was a weird sense of unreality in being thoroughly kissed while riding a horse on the lap of a man, she decided as his mouth came warmly down on to hers and parted her lips without really having to coax them much. The sun beat warmly down on their two heads, and the smell of horse, heat and man all culminated to hold her encapsulated in the sheer pleasure of the kiss.

'You know, *caro*,' he murmured thoughtfully as his mouth drew slowly away from hers, 'there is one solution open to us which would solve all our problems. You could marry me, Cassandra, and make this your permanent home from now on.'

CHAPTER EIGHT

JARRED violently out of her sensual haze, Cass just stared at Carlo. 'W-what did you say?' she whispered breathlessly.

'You heard me, *caro*,' he mocked her stunned expression. 'I am asking you to marry me.'

'But th-that's ridiculous!' she gasped, jerking stiffly upright on his lap when something inside her began to flutter desperately. 'What kind of solution is that?' she added shrilly.

'The ideal one to soothe Teresa's feelings of insecurity,' he murmured quietly, beginning to frown at her obvious agitation.

'By swapping one set of problems for another set?' she cried, then shook her head. 'No,' she said. 'The idea is absolutely not on. As I said—it's ridiculous.'

'Why is it?' he demanded, grimly pulling the horse to a halt so that he could give her his full attention. 'We—care something for one another, Cassandra—no! You cannot deny it!' he insisted when she went to do just that. 'Physically we are perfect for each other—something else you cannot deny!' he put in before she tried to deny that one as well. 'We both want the same things where Teresa is concerned—her happiness and our own peace of mind that we are giving her the best love and care life can offer her. Why should the idea of you and I marrying to give her that seem so ridiculous to you?'

'Why?' she repeated distractedly. God, was the man totally insensitive where she was concerned? Couldn't he see—didn't he know that it was herself she was trying to protect here, and not Teresa? She was in love with him—dammit! Madly, stupidly, inconsolably in love with the father of her sister's child! With the man who had offered Elizabeth nothing—none of this!

She shook her head again, the guilty torment going on inside her showing in the stark white tension in her face, and Carlo sighed in angry exasperation. 'Oh, come on, Cassandra,' he muttered impatiently. 'I can't believe you are this shocked. What do you think I have been leading up to during the last two weeks? Of course the obvious answer has always been that you and I marry to give Teresa the stability she needs in her life!'

Further shock because he had actually been planning this all along had her eyes widening in her pale face. Then she was breaking free from his grasp, pushing his detaining arm away from her with trembling fingers, and braving the daunting height she was seated at to scramble down from the horse's back. They were only a few hundred yards away from the house. Terri was already there; Cass could see one of Carlo's men helping the child out of the saddle, their light-hearted voices filtering towards her on the sultry air. Icy cold with re-action, she walked the few yards which brought her to the edge of the river.

It was a moment or two before he came to stand beside her, the horses set free to graze on the grassy bank behind them.

'I must assume by your response,' he drawled, 'that the idea does not appeal to you.'

He sounded very mocking, but Cass caught the sarcasm in his voice and knew she had probably stunned him with her reaction as much as he had stunned her with his proposal.

He must have been very sure of himself—very sure of her.

And why not? she thought bleakly. He is everything a man should be: tall, dark and undeniably handsome.

The deep brown colour of his eyes made her melt inside, the allure of his too, too sensual mouth was a constant torment to her. He was a good father—she had already seen the evidence of that in the quiet, firm, loving way he treated Terri. He would be a loyal husband, too. The way he spoke of his first wife showed he possessed a deep sense of responsibility towards those he cared for.

And as a lover?

She quivered, weak feelings of need almost overwhelming her. He was offering her his body and Teresa's happiness. But what about love? One night in his arms and any defences she had left against him would come tumbling down, making her his slave for life, while she was—what to him? The loving aunt and surrogate mother to his child? The woman he would treat with the respect a wife deserved, but little else?

No, it wasn't enough, and she refused to let herself be drawn into making that ultimate sacrifice. Not for him. Not even for Terri.

'I can't marry you, Carlo,' she stated flatly.

He let out an impatient sigh. 'Then what other solution do you see that will answer this dilemma we are now in?' he demanded. 'Are you perhaps intending separating the child from all who love her here by taking her back to England with you next week? And, if so, how will you explain to her why you are doing such a cruel thing? How?' He took hold of her by the shoulders to bring her in front of him. He was angry, his mouth, so recently softened by hers, tight now and hard. 'How will you explain to her, *caro*, that on finding a father who loves her she now has to say goodbye to him?'

'She has not accepted that you do love her, yet,' Cass reminded him.

'And will never do so while she believes I hold merely a transient role in her life!' His harsh sigh ripped like a pain right through her. 'Teresa needs me, Cassandra,' he continued grimly. 'She may not understand how much yet, but she needs the strength and stability only a loving father can offer her. And I think you know it.'

Oh, yes, she knew it. She had known it from the moment she had arrived in this beautiful place and seen just what the child had been missing. Sighing heavily, she sent her eyes on a painful scan of the sweet-smelling glory of his beautiful valley. It was all here—everything a child could possibly want from life. And out there beyond it spread the world this man had the resources to lay at Teresa's feet.

'Can you do it?' Carlo persisted harshly. 'Can you bring yourself to separate her from all of this?'

Of course she couldn't. She could not deprive Terri of any of it.

Not even for Liz's sake.

Liz... Cass's heart quivered on an ever-present sensation of gut-curdling guilt where her sister was concerned. Liz could have shared all this with them. Liz had possessed the right to share it all.

'Or,' he pushed on relentlessly, 'do you still intend putting the child through the trauma of choosing for herself?'

'God, no!' She even shuddered at the idea. Then, dragging in a painful breath of air, she looked up at him and forced herself to say what she had known for a long time now, had to be said. 'When I leave here next week, I won't be taking Terri with me,' she told him. 'Y-you are quite right,' she went on thickly. 'I don't have the right to deny her all of this.' Her vision blurred by the sudden onset of tears, and she blinked them angrily away. 'Once—once I'm out of the way, she'll come to accept you, Carlo, I'm sure of it. Sh-she's bound to be happier here with you than she could be with me.'

'Oh, yes,' he jeered, 'she will be absolutely elated to watch you walk out of her life—my God, Cassandra!'

he exploded. 'Haven't you been listening to a single word I have been saying? I could no more condone separating you from Teresa than I could——'

'Taking a baby from its mother's womb?'

The words were out before Cass could stop them, and they hung in the air between them, saying so much that neither of them had the power to ignore them.

Carlo turned away from her in a way that cut right into her because she knew she had just wounded him with that cruelly uncalculated thrust. 'So, we are back to your damned sister,' he muttered.

'And the mother of your child!' Cass flared, instantly on the defensive at his derisive tone.

'Wasn't she just?' he clipped, then turned back to face her, his eyes so hard now that they looked like black marble in his taut face. 'I'm warning you, Cassandra,' he went on grimly, 'I won't see Teresa hurt by anyone, and that includes you. I don't care what it takes, but you will stay here voluntarily with us or, so help me, I'll find a way to make you.'

'Blackmail again, *signore*?' His threat was enough to bring the sparks leaping from her sea green eyes. 'Knowing what I do about you, I suppose I should have expected you'd revert to form the moment I tried to oppose you!' Yet she hadn't, and it hurt her love for him to know he could still threaten her—though she didn't show it, her chin lifting in proud defiance of everything, including her thankless feelings of love! 'What are you intending to do,' she challenged bitterly, 'use your filthy file about my sister again?'

'No.' Reaching for her again, his grip was painful as he dragged her angrily against him. 'Use this!' he growled, and brought his mouth forcefully down on to hers.

He meant to punish her for her quick, acid tongue, and, certainly, the kiss was hard and angry, yet the moment their mouths met the passion flared like a burning furnace between them, and within seconds they were straining against each other, their tongues locked, breath ragged, senses spinning away on a complete collapse of everything sane.

It was he who drew away first, holding her upright with his hard hands while his eyes flicked contemptuously over her dazed and quivering body.

'Sexual blackmail is infinitely more enjoyable, don't you agree, *caro*?' he taunted cruelly, then abruptly let go of her to walk away, leaving her breathless and swaying, the heat of utter humiliation burning inside her.

He was out to dinner that night—thank God. Because Cass wasn't sure she could just sit calmly at the same table as him and pretend nothing was wrong in front of his mother, when really she wanted to fly at him with her nails.

From hating to liking to loving him, she had now reverted to hating him again. Mrs Valenti kept on looking curiously at her, though she forbore to ask just what had happened to send her son slamming out of the house only an hour after they returned from their ride, and why Cassandra was looking more hostile now than she had done on her first day here.

The next morning was no better. Over breakfast they exchanged the barest essentials in social manners, and then only for Terri's sake. The child was excited about their sea trip today, and thankfully not even the ire sparking from one adult to the other seemed to pierce her happy anticipation.

Guido was already waiting for them when they arrived at the quay, standing on a natty white speed launch which was to take them out to the yacht.

'Ah, the lovely Teresa!' he exclaimed as Carlo handed his daughter down to him. 'So we meet at last! My name is Guido, and I demand a kiss before I will let you come sailing with me!'

'You're silly!' the child giggled, but gave him the kiss anyway, before wriggling to be put down.

And Guido turned his attention on Cass. 'I am at your service, Miss Marlow,' he said, holding out his hand to help her into the launch. 'You look even more beautiful than you did the first time I saw you.' He smiled his wickedly teasing smile.

'Talking of beauties,' Carlo drawled from the quay, 'has Sabrina arrived yet?'

'Sabrina, arrive on time, Carlo?' his manager mocked. 'You are the optimist, my friend.'

'She was warned not to be late for this trip,' Carlo grunted as he stepped down on to the launch.

Just then, a bright red sports car pulled up at the quay, and Sabrina Reducci stepped into view.

'Ah, Guido!' she smiled as she reached the launch. 'Come to watch over our landlubbers, have you? Mmm, but it is a perfect day for sailing, is it not?' She landed lightly at Guido's feet. 'There is just enough breeze to put a swell on the sea, and make for an interesting trip.'

Was she hoping they were the seasick type? Cass wondered. Well, she could well be right, she then conceded. They had never been on the sea before to find out!

'See, *amico*, we are colour-co-ordinated today!' With her usual expertise, Sabrina brought everyone's attention honing on to her exquisite figure encased in designer navy blue Bermudas and white shirt that made Cass feel almost slovenly in the baggy old white T-shirt and pale blue shorts she had flung on over her simple white one-piece swimsuit.

Then Sabrina's arms were around Carlo's neck, and the usual kissing routine began, her lush lips moving from one tanned cheek to the other before coming to rest on Carlo's mouth, while he accepted it with a smiling indulgence that made Cass's blood boil.

Love is for lovers, my foot! she thought angrily, and went to stand next to Terri by the rail. Love is for anyone who'll kiss the man!

'The scowl does not go with the day, *caro*.' At the low, soft sound of that mocking voice, Cass glanced around to find Guido studying her curiously. 'This is supposed to be a "pleasure" cruise.'

Is it? she wondered derisively. Some hope.

The crewman at the helm of the launch got them under way with a deep roar from the powerful engine, saving her from having to reply as they went speeding away from the quay and out into the clear blue waters of the bay. Ten minutes later they had clambered aboard Carlo's luxury yacht, and his captain, Tarazona, after being formally introduced to them, was inviting Teresa on to his bridge to watch them sail out.

Excited by the idea, she became his instant friend, tucking her hand into his and going off with him without a second thought.

Feeling suddenly out of her depth without her faithful companion by her side, Cass hovered behind the others as they filed inside for drinks, then turned to lean on the rail instead of following them, preferring to remain outside and—childishly, perhaps—watch the boat sail out.

Her legs were in the shade, protected by an overhang from the deck above, but her arms and face were fully exposed to the heat of the morning sun, then, as they began to move, the breeze caught at her hair, flipping it out behind her as she turned her face into it.

It was an exhilarating sensation, and slowly some of the tension she had been suffering with since the afternoon before began to seep out of her muscles on the soothing hiss of the water as they cut a sleek line through its aquamarine depths, and she watched San Remo grow smaller and smaller, its bright white walls and red roof-tops slowly merging behind a haze of shimmering heat.

Then she suddenly wasn't alone, a muscled brown arm lightly covered with silky black hair coming to rest on the rail barely half an inch away from her own, and she snapped to attention, the smile she had managed to relax into gone in a moment.

Her reaction made his jaw clench. 'Easy, *amore*,' Carlo drawled sardonically. 'I am not contaminated in any way, you know.'

'I never thought you were!' she denied, turning her face away from him.

'No?' he mocked. 'I know I shocked you with my proposal yesterday, but I never once considered you might be so offended by it that you can barely stand me near you.'

'I was not offended.' She was forced into making the second denial. Then found herself wondering if one of the many angry emotions cluttering up her insides did spring from a sense of deep offence at his proposal. After all, did any woman find pleasure in knowing she had been proposed to simply to solve a pressing problem?

'Then do you think you could at least look at me while we talk?' he suggested. 'Lovely though your hair is, loose and flowing like that, I would much rather look at your beautiful face.'

The husky appeal in his voice rippled over the fine layers of her skin, causing a hot tingling in the pit of her stomach that had her clenching the muscles in an effort to quell the instant reminder of how easily he could make her sexually aware of him.

'We tried talking yesterday, and look where it got us.' Her tone was bitter. 'I don't know what it is you really want from me any more, Carlo,' she whispered bleakly.

'I don't think I ever did.' Suddenly, she found herself having to fight against a hot bank of tears.

'I want you!' he muttered. 'I want my daughter—and myself—to be happy together. Is it really too much to ask that you marry me to achieve those things?'

Much, much too much. 'Do people find happiness in a marriage of convenience?' she threw at him tartly.

'Oh, no, Cassandra——' he shook his dark head in denial of that remark '—there is nothing even remotely convenient in the way I constantly ache for you. In fact——' he grimaced, setting the nerves jumping all over her body when he reached up to stroke gently the bright tendrils of her wind-blown hair away from her pale, tense cheek '—it is damned inconvenient most of the time.'

'Don't!' She twisted her head in an attempt to dislodge his caressing fingers.

'Don't what?' he asked. 'Don't force you to accept that you feel the exact same way about me? How else am I supposed to get through to you when you're so damned stubborn?'

'I'm not stubborn!' she snapped, at last turning to glare at him. 'I'm just...' But the words died in her throat, locked there by the look of hungry intent she saw glowing in his eyes.

'No,' she choked. But he ignored her, his hand curving beneath the billowing flow of her hair to grasp her nape.

Instantly, his touch set her senses tingling, and she began to tremble. His eyes, darkening by the second, were drawing her into a deep, swirling promise of passion. Heat poured into her cheeks, then into her lips until they parted, full and throbbing. And Carlo muttered something violent beneath his breath.

'Stubborn,' he repeated huskily, 'but so damned beautiful.' And he pulled her mouth on to his.

It wasn't fair! she thought wretchedly as a hot tide of excitement went coursing through her that had her sagging weakly against him.

Reacting, Carlo shifted his position, folding her in his strong embrace and pressing her back against the rail so that she had no choice but to feel the tightening evidence of his own instant arousal.

'Cassandra, I want you,' he murmured, and robbed the breath from her body when he slid his hands beneath her loose T-shirt, and began following a sensual path along her slender contours until he found and cupped her rounded breasts. Beneath their covering of thin white Lycra, her nipples hardened beneath his kneading hands, sending out a spray of tingling pleasure to every corner of her body, and she arched in wild response.

'No!' Cass groaned deliriously.

His mouth smothered the protest with a long, searching kiss that was all the more potent for his obvious urgency. And she surrendered weakly, her hands creeping along his arm and across the bunching muscles of his shoulders until they found and lost themselves in the silken darkness of his hair.

A seagull, screeching overhead, broke them jerkily apart. And, through a red-hot haze of shock and passion, they just stared at each other. Both trembling, both gasping for breath. Both so acutely aroused that there was a chance that if anyone touched them they would be electrocuted by the static emanating from them.

'Deny that if you dare,' Carlo muttered roughly when eventually he found the strength to speak.

She couldn't, and she knew it. 'But sex isn't everything,' she mumbled defensively.

'No,' he agreed. 'But it gives a marriage one hell of an advantage to begin on.'

'And love?' she asked in desperate agitation. 'Doesn't the lack of love between us matter to you at all?'

He stiffened, as if the question had stung him somehow. And his eyes snapped into a look of irritation. 'We both love Teresa. That should be enough, surely?'

No, it wasn't enough. Not for her, anyway. Not while she loved him, because it made her feel left right out in the cold. Sighing, she went to turn away, but he stopped her, his hand curving around her nape so that his thumb could gently lift her chin.

'If it bothers you this much, *caro*, then I promise we will take our time—go at your pace. I am no sex-crazed animal,' he said, then added on a wry grimace that made her heart flip over, 'Well, maybe a little crazed. But I will promise you this one thing. If you agree to marry me, Cassandra, I will do everything within my power to make you happy. It means that much to me. Think about it,' he huskily advised, 'because I am not going to give up on this. I am that determined, you understand?'

Leaning forwards, he pressed a last short but telling kiss to her throbbing mouth, then turned and walked away, leaving Cass leaning weakly against the yacht's rail.

He was beginning to get to her. To really, really get to her. Should she just give in, and simply let him devour her?

And it would be a devouring, she confessed. A complete and utter consuming of her soul.

Turning sluggishly, she lifted her hot face into the cooling breeze and closed her eyes, wondering bleakly just what she was going to do.

'You conniving little bitch!' A shrill voice jarred at her eardrums at the same time as a talon-like hand curled tightly around her arm.

Cass swung around in bewildered shock. 'I'm sorry?' she said, finding herself staring into Sabrina's hostile face.

'Do not play the innocent with me, you bitch!' Sabrina bit out at Cass's blank look. 'I know exactly what you are playing at! And I think it is time someone told you it is not going to work!'

Was she mad? Cass wondered bewilderedly, not knowing what she was talking about.

'Carlo is mine!' she spat. 'And you can taunt him with your sexy body and drive him wild with hunger for you—but in the end he will still be mine!' The violence written on her face was alarming. A green-eyed jealousy spitting venom at her. 'I have put in too many years of patience waiting for him to decide to take another wife simply to stand by and watch a cunning little bitch like you step in and steal him from me.' The fierce digging in of Sabrina's nails into her arm had Cass gasping in pain. 'So be warned, Miss Marlow,' she continued menacingly, 'you are playing a dangerous game. And I would take care that someone does not take steps to ensure your removal from it!'

With that, and while Cass was still floundering from the unexpected attack, Sabrina unclipped her nails from Cass's arm and turned to stalk away, leaving Cass shiveringly aware that she had just been seriously threatened.

'What was all that about?' Guido came up, his usual smile nowhere to be seen as he watched Sabrina go. He turned to look curiously at Cass, then frowned when he saw her deathly pallor. 'Watch her, Cassandra,' he warned grimly. 'Sabrina is what we would call *una patella*—like the limpet,' he explained, 'she latches on to her quarry and holds on tight. It will take a sharp implement and a lot of force to prise her free.'

Cass's hand went up to cover her arm where Sabrina's nails had dug into her skin, and another shiver rippled through her. Unknowingly, Guido had just described Sabrina exactly—and Cass had the marks to prove it.

'Y-you sound as if you don't like her very much,' she murmured absently.

'She is beautiful enough,' he allowed, 'but too—obsessive for my tastes.' He gave a lazy shrug as if in dismissal of something which did not interest him much, and changed the subject. 'I came to see if I could perhaps tempt you to have that drink now,' he invited with his sunny smile back in place.

Pulling herself together, Cass went willingly enough, but she was quiet for most of their sail around the coast, keeping her attention almost exclusively fixed on her niece, who was eager to explore every inch of the yacht.

They anchored off a tiny secluded bay where a half-circle of golden sand was backed by the high sun-bleached cliff-face, making it inaccessible from any other route but the sea. It was here they were to swim before they had lunch. And Cass shyly removed her T-shirt and shorts, and hurriedly slid off the diving platform into the cool, clear water before Sabrina could further unsettle her by running her condescending gaze over her old-fashioned halter-neck style costume. The other woman was wearing a skimpy one-piece of bright fluorescent pink which set off her tan—and showed more than it covered with its waist-high cut-away sides and low-dipping front and back.

Sabrina dived off the side of the boat to enter the water with hardly a splash. 'I wish I could do that,' Terri murmured enviously, treading water with her small chin stuck up in the air while Cass stayed watchfully close to her. The child's in-built fearlessness of water was very commendable, but she had a tendency to be a danger to herself if she wasn't watched.

Carlo entered the water by the same impressive route as Sabrina, followed quickly by Guido, and, within seconds, Cass could see the three dark heads striking out in a smooth line for the shore. She sighed heavily—not because she wished she was with them, but because she knew she did not swim that well or that gracefully. A once-a-week splash in the local public swimming-baths back home did not lend itself to strong swimming—not among the crush of other users in the pool, anyway.

But she and Terri had always enjoyed their weekly play in the water, and that was what they did now, swimming and teasing each other, dipping and diving, always close enough to the diving platform for Cass to heave Terri on to it if she got tired. And for a few precious minutes she was able to forget all the problems assailing her in the comforting delight of Terri's high antics.

So she let go with a high-pitched scream when something warm and alive suddenly swam between her legs and lifted her high on its broad shoulders. Terri swished around in the water with a startled look on her face, then the wretched child was laughing when she encountered Carlo's face grinning at her from between her aunt's golden thighs.

'Put me down, you brute!' Cass cried, her fingers clutching at the wet silk thickness of his hair.

'Down?' he said. 'OK,' and casually tossed her off behind him. She flailed like a beached whale for a moment, gasping and spluttering.

Completely forgetting the tension between them, the desire to get her own back was too tempting to ignore. And with the green flash from her eyes the only warning he was going to get, but one Terri recognised with a squeal of delight, she dived beneath the water and found his feet, tugging him down into the crystal-clear depths with her lungs full enough with air to keep her down for a long time while she didn't care less if Carlo drowned. What she and Terri couldn't do with long, lithe swimming strokes, they could certainly do within the

confines of a small space of water. And she turned to
grin at him as she let go of his foot, air bubbles escaping
from between her even white teeth. Above their heads,
Terri had her face stuck into the water to watch the game,
her little legs paddling like mad to keep her afloat. Carlo
glanced up, saw the little girl, and made a nodding re-
quest at Cass, who gave permission to do his worst.

With the lean, lithe stretch of his dark golden body,
he struck for the surface, and, as Cass watched from
her position beneath the water, Carlo arrived between
Terri's legs, giving her the same treatment he had given
Cass.

By the time the child landed in a huge splash of water
behind him, Cass was striking for the surface, her lungs
beginning to burst for air. She came up beside a flailing
Terri, intending to gather her into her arms, only to find
Guido had got there before her, and was already carrying the giggling child away, leaving Cass alone with
Carlo treading water close by, still grinning.

Further away, Cass noticed a dark head bobbing in
the water. Sabrina's hard gaze was fixed on her. And
once again that feeling of threat assailed Cass, and she
lifted her hand to the faded marks on her arm, going
cold inside suddenly.

Glancing at her, Carlo went still also, his eyes narrowing as he followed her pensive stare. 'She—worries
you, Cassandra?' he asked.

Cass blinked, sending him a brief rueful smile. 'No
more than usual, I suppose,' she dismissed, but knew
she did not sound sincere, and Carlo frowned at her for
a moment, before pulling her close and kissing her fully
and seriously on her quivering lips.

'Sabrina means nothing to me—nothing,' he stated
huskily. 'You understand, *caro*?' His dark brows arched
at her, and, flushing in confusion, she swam away.

She'd had more than enough play for one day.

They lunched beneath a canvas awning pulled across the sun-deck. Then Terri looked tired, and Cass gently suggested that the child might like to take a nap in one of the cabins below deck. The novelty appealed to the little girl, and she went down happily enough.

By the time Cass came back on deck, dressed in her T-shirt and shorts again, Carlo and Sabrina were stretched out next to each other in the sun, Sabrina lying flat on her back while Carlo leaned over her. They were talking quietly, almond eyes serious on Carlo as she listened intently to him.

So much for his earlier vow! Cass thought angrily as a pang of burning jealousy had her turning her face away from them. She sank down on one of the soft, cushioned loungers, curling her knees up to her chin to watch the passing scenery as the yacht moved slowly out to sea again. Her heart was actually hammering with resentment, body trembling with a possessive desire to go and break them up.

'The little one is asleep?' A hand appeared in her vision, holding out a tall, clear glass of something refreshing.

'Yes.' She smiled at Guido, accepting the glass from him. 'She will be annoyed later that she missed some of the trip, but if she doesn't take a nap she becomes unfit to know.'

He sat down on the end of her lounger, his tanned chest only slightly less impressive than his employer's. 'I was well and truly hooked by Carlo the first time we met, wasn't I?' he grimaced at Cass. 'You are no more Teresa's *mamma* than I am!'

She laughed, remembering the look on his face when Carlo had made that implication. 'What gave him away?' she asked.

'Your name did it,' he informed her, adding curiously, 'You are nothing like your sister, are you?

Elizabeth Marlow was at least three inches taller than you, and her hair was the palest natural blonde I have ever seen, and her eyes were blue, not green.'

'You knew Liz?' The surprise showed in her voice. Then she remembered that it was while on location here that her sister met Carlo.

He nodded his dark head. 'Your sister died last year,' he recalled, glancing up to catch the sudden bleakness cloud her sea-green gaze. 'I'm sorry,' he apologised immediately. 'I should not have mentioned it; it is clear the bereavement still brings you pain.'

At that moment, there was a sound of a scuffle, and both Cass and Guido glanced up in time to see Sabrina scramble to her feet. Her beautiful face white with anger, she paused, bending to whisper something harsh to Carlo, who just shrugged his broad, tanned shoulders and did not reply. Then she was glaring at Cass, and the look was so viciously malevolent that Cass gasped.

'My God,' Guido breathed as Sabrina stormed away, 'now what brought that on, I wonder...?'

Cass couldn't answer; she was trembling on the aftermath of that look.

'The wind is getting up.' Carlo's curt voice had their heads turning to find him on his feet studying the sudden change in the sky. 'Clouds are gathering on the horizon. We could be in for a storm. Guido, go and see what Captain Tarazona thinks, while I go and check Teresa. I don't want her frightened of the sea on her first excursion on to it.'

'I'll go, shall I?' Cass was already halfway off the lounger when Carlo stopped her as Guido moved off to speak to the captain.

'No, I'll do it,' he said, waving her back into her lounger then walking away, leaving her alone on the sundeck.

She sipped at her drink for a while, knees still tucked beneath her chin as she gazed out at the steadily darkening sky, reluctant to go inside if it meant she had to face more of Sabrina's malice. But eventually it got so cold that she had to get up, discarding her glass so that she could rub her bare arms with her hands as she moved to the stern of the boat, where the flimsy chain-link barrier gave access to the diving platform below, still reluctant to go inside.

A sudden gust of wind made her shiver, and she glanced up, surprised to see how quickly the clouds had come upon them, lying black and ugly right above the yacht. The first smattering of rain sprayed into her face, and out to sea white horses were chasing each other across the tops of the waves, and she could feel the difference in the rocking action of the yacht beneath her feet.

Then the rain became a sudden deluge, and she turned quickly, intent on getting inside before she was thoroughly soaked through to the bone. But as she moved the yacht made a sudden lurch when a wave hit it side on, and she staggered, reaching out to grab at the first thing that came to hand. The chain-link barrier swung violently with her weight, and she cried out in alarm when she realised what she had done.

'Cassandra!' someone yelled out. Then, 'Sabrina! Stop her for God's sake!'

But by then the chain link was already swinging giddily away from her, and the last thing Cass heard, as her own body weight took her toppling helplessly over the side of the yacht, was Terri's shrill voice screaming, 'Daddy——!'

CHAPTER NINE

CASS hit the water just beyond the lethal spin of the yacht's propeller, but the turbulence it was leaving in its wake sucked her downwards in a swirling mass of foaming bubbles. Shocked and disorientated, she had no choice but to go with the violent pull, spiralling downwards with her arms and legs flailing in a useless effort to slow her downward progress. Panic rattled at her senses, the real fear that she was going to drown congealing the blood in her veins. Her lungs were threatening to burst in their need for air, her heart pounding, the fast, erratic beat thundering in her ears. And it seemed like long, terrifying minutes before her own natural buoyancy began to slow her down, then pure instinct had her making a desperate strike for the surface, which seemed a long, long way above her head.

She broke the surface just in time to receive the hard smack of a wave to the side of her face. Her mouth, already open to release the pressure inside her lungs, filled with salty water, and she choked, her head going under again.

She didn't know it, but she was being tossed around in the turbulent wash from the yacht. A yacht she could see neither sight nor sign of as she came up for a second time to peer frantically about her.

Oh, God, she pleaded wretchedly, come back—come back!

How long did it take a yacht of that size to turn full circle? Wildly treading water, she found herself recalling lurid stories of the big liners needing miles to make such a manoeuvre. Another wave broke over her, and as she came up coughing and spluttering she felt a sharp pain on the side of her head, and vaguely remembered hitting it on something as she went over the side. The diving platform, probably, she decided hazily, already beginning to tire at trying to keep herself afloat.

The waves were roughening, the sky black above her head, the rain pouring from it so heavy that it made it all the more difficult to draw in air. The salty water kept slapping at her face, and her head was throbbing painfully, cold striking into her which had to be a mixture of exposure and shock. Don't panic! she told herself fiercely as yet more salty water stung into her eyes and mouth, making her choke again as she gulped it into her lungs.

Something wet and alive brushed by her, and she screamed, sinking beneath the water as terror snaked through the shivering layers of her icy flesh. A strong arm came beneath her shoulders, yanking her to the surface again. And, choking violently, she opened her stinging eyes to stare in horror at Carlo's grim, wet face.

'Carlo,' she gasped. 'Oh, God!' Her arms, heavy with weariness, flailed through the water to grip tightly around him.

'Easy,' his rough voice rasped, 'I have you. Hang on to me and get your breath back. I have you safe, *amore*, I have you...'

Cass pressed her face into the hollow of his shoulder; it felt wet and cold, but so incredibly real, the arm he had clamped around her waist a solid force she willingly gave herself up to as she groaned in throbbing relief.

'Hey——' he was attempting to sound light despite the hectic heaving of his lungs '—don't you faint on me!' he commanded, even managing a small laugh as he added ruefully, 'This is neither the time nor the place for it, *caro*.'

'Don't faint,' she repeated dizzily, and he laughed again, his mouth sliding across her cold, wet cheek.

Beneath the surface, the water swirled and eddied around their limbs as they laboriously trod water, while above them the water boiled and slapped, tossing them about as if they were matchsticks. And the rain poured down on them, cutting visibility down to nothing and closing them into the soulless world of a cruel, cold sea.

What was he doing here? Cass suddenly asked herself, lifting her face to frown in confusion at the fierce tension locked on to his features. Surely he hadn't fallen overboard too?

A wave hit them full on, splitting them apart and sending them both under and struggling back to the surface. Cass cried out, her fingers groping out blindly in search of him, their fingers touched, and Carlo clung on to her, drawing her towards him, twisting her around and dragging her backwards against his chest, his arm a solid clamp again, his shoulder a cushion for her pounding head.

'My head hurts,' she groaned, then did what he had expressly asked her not to do, and blacked out to the sound of his muttered curses when he saw the thick red blood oozing from a wound to one side of her head.

She awoke to the cool, crisp feel of hospital linen pinning her down to a high, narrow bed. How she knew she was in hospital she didn't know because her eyes certainly refused to open to check the theory. Her head was throbbing, and it felt as though every muscle in her body was sore and stiff. Her mouth felt like sandpaper, and she tried to lick her cracked and dried lips only to find the effort too much, and groaned weakly in frustration.

Immediately a hand touched her brow, long fingers deliciously cooling against her burning skin. 'Cassandra?'

The voice was familiar, and she frowned at it, trying to put a face to the sound. It wouldn't come, and she sighed, wishing she weren't feeling so utterly used up.

'Drink,' she managed to croak, and the hand was removed, only to come back almost immediately to curve around the back of her neck.

'Easy, *amore*,' the same deep voice she had taken with her into the blackness warned. 'Just wet your lips for now. And try not to move your head too much.'

Her head? Cass allowed some of the water to trickle on to her tongue, then lay back against the hand, exhausted just by that small exertion.

'Carlo?' she whispered faintly, the reference to her head for some reason giving her a connection to the voice, or maybe it was the gentle strength of the hand holding her.

'*Si, mi amore*, it is I...'

Her fingers fluttered, itching to search out his hand, but too weak to try. As if he sensed her need, his hand closed warmly around hers, and she sighed contentedly, feeling safe—safe and...

Sleep overtook her in a single moment, and the next time she awoke she managed to open her heavy eyes to find the smiling dark face of a stranger standing over her. He was holding her wrist, his gaze fixed on the face of his gold wristwatch. When he noticed her looking at him, he smiled. 'Ah, back with the living, *signorina*, and about time too.'

'Where——?'

'Where are you?' The man, who was obviously a doctor, gave a long-suffering sigh. 'I do wish my concussed patients would come up with something more interesting when they awaken from a coma; but——' he put down her wrist, and produced a pencil-thin torch which he proceeded to shine into her protesting eyes '—you are in hospital of course,' he informed her while concentrating on examining her eyes. 'You enjoy swimming in stormy seas, *signorina*?' he then drily enquired as he straightened up again.

The storm. Everything came flooding back. The yacht, the change in weather, her stupid slip at the stern of the boat and her even more stupid action in reaching out for something as flimsy as a piece of chain to save her. She remembered the anxious call, and a hazy impression that someone was coming up behind her, then the fall, the horrible heart-clamouring fall into the swirling sea.

'I banged my head,' she recalled frowningly, and at last she moved, slowly bringing her hand up to touch the side of her head, which was now swathed in bandages.

'You did,' the doctor agreed. 'You banged your head, almost drowned, drank too much salt-water, gave yourself a dose of pneumonia, and worried everyone that you might just decide to expire after all the trouble they had gone to stop you drowning in the sea.'

'Carlo?' Fear crawled along her veins, her green eyes stark with it as she stared anxiously at the doctor.

He grimaced. 'I presume you are referring to that gentleman who has been haunting the corridor outside this room as if he was afraid you might disappear if he did not keep a constant vigil on you?' he mocked. 'He is fine,' he assured.

Cass smiled, making a hazy link with the doctor's joke and Carlo's previous experience of her annoying ability to disappear. 'He pulled me out, didn't he?' she frowned, trying to remember the final stages of her ordeal, but couldn't, only Carlo's arm coming so strongly around her, then—nothing.

'No, a rescue helicopter pulled you both out,' the doctor corrected, smiling at her startled look. 'Mr Valenti simply held you above water until they got you—though how he managed it is still beyond anyone's comprehension.' His dark head shook ruefully. 'The storm took a decidedly nasty turn, and it took the rescue teams over an hour to find you both. And the only discomfort he received from the ordeal was a slight chill! Ah——' the head shook again '—some men have all the luck. And that one has more than his fair share, since he got to save the lovely damsel in distress in true heroic fashion, and escapes himself with only a slight chill for his trouble! And even that did not dare linger long,' he finished on a sigh. 'Three days and he had shrugged it arrogantly away!'

Something thumped in Cass's breast. 'How long have I been here?' she asked jerkily.

'Almost a week,' she was informed, and the sheer shock of the answer brought her jerking upright in the n-

wise action set her head reeling, her body
he   g, and had the doctor reaching out to take hold
a⁺   Now that was foolish, *signorina*,' he scolded as
ly laid her back down again. 'You are to lie there
y without jumping about like that.'

t I have to get up!' she gasped out frantically. 'I
 to——'

'You will be going nowhere, Cassandra,' a deep voice
ruded on the proceedings. And she squinted through
pain hitting at the back of her eyes towards the man
who had just entered the room, seeing only his blurred outline.

'Carlo,' she murmured thickly, then thoroughly embarrassed herself by breaking down and sobbing. Sobbing weakly, pathetically, crying like a baby.

His arms came around her, the bed sinking as he sat down beside her, and through the sudden flood of delayed shock she heard him clipping out questions to the doctor, who was defending himself in the tones of one who was bewildered by the sudden outburst.

But he didn't understand—couldn't understand—what this full week's oblivion meant to her!

'Hey...' A gentle voice murmured by her ear, and it was only then that she realised that she and Carlo were alone, the doctor banished, most likely, by a man who thought it his right to take control of anything he wished—even a hospital patient. 'This is no way to greet your saviour! I am a hero in this place, and here you are, ruining my newly acquired image by weeping at the sight of me!'

'But I've got to get up!' she insisted dazedly. 'M-my job—I have to——'

'God in heaven, woman!' he bit out roughly, dropping the indulgent tone and easily quelling her weak attempt at pulling away from him. 'Have you any idea of the worry you have put us all through? And all you are co cerned with is your damned job!'

'I—I'm sorry,' she choked. But there was no way could understand; nobody could know how vital th job link with England was to her. It was her escape rou the place for her to go to lick her wounds when all this between them was over.

'Cassandra,' he sighed, taking pity on her, a dropping the harsh tone, 'you have not to worry yourse about anything. I promise you, I will take care everything.'

'I owe you enough already,' she whispered, opening her eyes to look at him, the fine-veiled lids heavy with tiredness. 'Y-you shouldn't have risked your life for me like that,' she added awkwardly. 'Poor Terri must have been out of her mind with fear for both of us.'

Carlo grimaced. 'She was,' he admitted, laying her gently back against the pillows. 'I don't think she will easily forgive either of us for almost dying on her.'

'She's taken enough in her little life,' Cass whispered, remembering Liz, and how devastated the poor child had been at losing her mother. 'She deserves better,' she added sombrely.

'Yes,' he sighed. 'But for now we will concentrate on your welfare and not Teresa's,' he determined firmly, coming suddenly to his feet. Then surprised Cass by leaning over to press a warm, hard kiss to her mouth. 'Leave everything to me about the job,' he commanded gruffly. 'I shall see what I can do.'

Then he was walking swiftly for the door with his husky, 'Goodnight, *amore*,' still echoing warmly in her mind as she dropped smoothly into sleep.

She slept all the way through to the morning afterwards. But where her earlier sleep had been her body's way of shutting down to aid her recovery, she now slept the sleep of the restful, and awoke the next morning feeling refreshed and one hundred per cent better.

She was up and wrapped in a soft white towelling robe, sitting in a chair by the open window, when the door opened and Terri bowled in, dragging on the arm of a puffing Maria.

'Cass!' the child cried, breaking free so that she could launch herself across the room and on to her aunt.

Cass winced as the little girl landed sobbing on her lap, her tender muscles not ready for such rough treatment, but a single glance at the child's white little face and she gathered her close, careless of how much she hurt because it was clear that Terri had been hurting longer.

'I thought y-you w-was going to die!' she sobbed into Cass's throat, the broken words tumbling over each other to get out while her grip was strangling around her aunt's neck. 'An' w-we couldn't s-see you or my daddy...'

Daddy? Cass picked up sharply on the word. Terri had just spoken of Carlo as her daddy!

'...And it r-rained an' it r-rained!' she was stammering on, unaware of her aunt's sudden stillness. 'And

Gu-Guido h-had to slap S-Sabrin-na's f-face to s-stop her screaming! And——'

'You were very brave and just stood very quietly beside the captain while he radioed for help in the search,' a calm voice put in.

Cass looked at Mrs Valenti over the top of Terri's curls. She was leaning heavily on her sticks, and looked as though she'd aged years since Cass last saw her. Maria was still by the door, wiping a tear from her eye. And Cass hugged the sobbing little girl closer.

'It has been a difficult time for her, Cassandra,' Mrs Valenti murmured quietly. 'A terrible ordeal, to have both you and Carlo go missing for a whole hour like that, and in the middle of such a shocking storm. Then this last week...' The old woman sighed expressively.

'But I'm fine now, darling,' Cass soothed the poor child. 'Your—your *daddy* looked after me until someone found us, and all I have left to show for all that fuss is a bump on my head the size of an egg!'

'Really, Cass?' Huge watery eyes lifted from her throat to stare at her in fascination. 'Can I see it?'

'Sure you can.' She bent her head down, just managing to stop the child touching the new bald patch she now sported, the size of a fifty-pence piece, where the doctors had stitched up the gash in her head.

'Ooh, Cass! That looks horrid!' the child exclaimed.

'It feels horrid too,' she ruefully agreed. Plus she hadn't much liked the sight of her lovely hair shorn away in a neat circle to one side of her crown. 'Better now, poppet?' she smiled.

Tears filled Terri's eyes again. 'I thought God had snatched you away and taken you up to heaven to be with Mummy,' she choked. 'And he can't do that, Cass,' she protested brokenly, 'or who will look after me?'

The daddy you've just acknowledged at last, Cass thought heavily.

'Teresa!' Mrs Valenti's voice was sharper than Cass
had ever heard her, and even Terri was surprised enough
to glance warily at her *nonna*, who was frowning scold-
ingly at her. 'Did your *papa* only let you come here today
on the promise that you do not upset your aunt?'

The curly head nodded glumly.

'Then give Cassandra that big kiss you've been saving
for her, and get down off her knee—or you will tire her
out so much that they will never let her out of here!'

Contrite, Terri did as she was told, giving Cass one
last huge hug and kiss, and whispering, 'I love you,
Cass,' before scrambling down.

'And I love you too, poppet,' Cass thickly replied,
still having to struggle with her own tears.

'Now,' Mrs Valenti continued briskly, 'if I give you
some *lire*...' a gnarled hand rested one stick against the
end of Cassandra's bed while she rummaged in her
pocket and came out with some money '... Maria will
take you for that ice-cream I promised you.'

Assured of the living proof of her aunt Cass's recovery, the child went happily to accept the money. And
with a smile and a, 'See you later,' she went willingly
into Maria's care, talking the servant's head off as they
walked from the room.

'Shoo!' Mrs Valenti sighed, moving stiffly over to the
chair near Cass to lower herself into it. 'I have to tell
you, Cassandra,' she said, 'she has been a handful
without you there to reassure her. She would accept
comfort from no one, not even her father.' She glanced
sharply at Cass. 'You noticed how she has at last accepted her *papa*?' the older woman asked carefully. 'In
a space of mere seconds, Cassandra, she saw her aunt
tumble over the side of the yacht in one direction, and
her *papa* dive over in another!' Carlo's mother shook
her silvered head. 'It is perhaps only natural that her

own defences should crumble at a time of such terrible stress, I suppose.'

Cass nodded mutely, feeling something heavy begin to press down on her heart, and she couldn't make up her mind if it was relief for what was, in effect, the last hurdle negotiated, or regret for what would never be again.

Terri was truly Carlo's daughter now, and for once and for all Cass allowed herself to accept that her own time here was definitely drawing to a close.

'But that is enough about my granddaughter,' Mrs Valenti inserted more brightly. 'How are you feeling now, my dear? We have all been very concerned for you...'

Later that afternoon, while Cass was resting in bed, Guido breezed into the room, his arms full of flowers. 'Fresh from the market this morning!' he announced, opening his arms to let the lovely blooms tumble carelessly all over the snowy white cover. Then, while Cass scolded him laughingly, he sat himself down on the bed and grasped one of her hands. 'I am glad to see you so recovered, Cassandra,' he said earnestly. 'That hour-long horror on the open sea is something I never wish to experience again! I thought we had lost both you and Carlo. One moment you were standing by the stern, the next gone!' He shook his sleek, dark head.

'I only had the chance to shout to Sabrina to try to catch you before you had disappeared! The next thing, Carlo is diving over the side, and the nightmare really began. The storm closed us in. I could see neither of you. Sabrina went into hysterics, and it took two of the crew and myself to get her down below while poor, brave Teresa remained supremely composed. "My daddy will find her," was all she said, and went calmly with the captain up on to the bridge to await the results. In all my life I have never seen such courage—and in one so small!'

Another shake of his head while Cass felt the lump of tears build in her throat once again. It wasn't bravery, she recognised wretchedly, it was Teresa refusing to accept the horror of what could really happen. Her vulnerable little heart just couldn't take the blow.

'How the hell Carlo found you is a mystery—even to him, I suspect.' He grimaced. 'And how the hell he kept you both afloat while the rescue services found you is another mystery! I know the man is strong,' he acknowledged mockingly, 'but does he have to be so damned invincible? It leaves no room for lesser mortals like me to shine!'

Her trail of visitors was apparently not over with Guido's exit. And she had just finished eating a light meal when the door opened yet again, and Sabrina Reducci, no less, walked in, looking nothing like the proud, contemptuous woman Cass had come to know.

She didn't look directly at Cass, but kept her eyes fixed on the white coverlet when she came to a standstill at the bottom of the bed. 'I—I am glad to see you recovering,' she murmured stiffly. 'It was an——'

'Ordeal, I know,' Cass put in a little wryly. She had come to accept that while she had been busy being in danger everyone else had been going through the biggest 'ordeal' of their lives. Unsure why Sabrina was here, and wary of her motives, Cass added carefully, 'I'm sorry I worried everybody so much. It was a stupid thing for me to do, to stand by that chain barrier when it was obvious the storm was right on us. I'm only glad nothing really tragic came out of it all—Carlo could have drowned, diving in after me like that...'

Sabrina shuddered, and Cass thought she'd hit on the real reason why she had come here. Was she blaming Cass for placing Carlo in such terrible danger? It could explain that strange look on the Italian girl's face.

'I could have stopped you falling!' she burst out suddenly, making Cass start. She stared at Sabrina, and was shocked by the look of guilt in those lush black eyes. 'I was standing there—right behind you, and I could have stopped you going over the side!'

Cass frowned, 'But, Sabrina, that would——'

'I did not because I did not want to save you!' she admitted wretchedly, cutting through what Cass had been going to say. 'I stood there thinking, If she drowns, Carlo will turn to me! And I did nothing to stop you falling—and now I feel so...!' Tears filled the beauty's eyes, and she shook her head, unable to go on.

Shocked by the confession, Cass just stared at her for a moment. Then sympathy welled up inside her, and she said gently, 'Sabrina, you didn't try to stop me falling because you *couldn't*,' she insisted. It was clear now that Sabrina had been having a hard struggle with her conscience since the incident began. 'If I couldn't stop myself from going in, then what chance did you have of stopping me? You would have been a fool if you had tried, because, if anything, I would have probably pulled you in too!'

'But Carlo said——'

'I don't care what Carlo said!' Cass interrupted impatiently. 'I was the one who slipped, I was the one who knew that nothing could have stopped that last lurch of the yacht which sent me over. I don't blame you for not racing to my rescue—in fact, I am relieved you didn't! I mean, what if you had drowned trying to save me? I would never have lived with myself! In fact,' she shuddered, 'it doesn't bear thinking about!'

A bleak smile touched the corners of Sabrina's pale lips. 'You are being very kind, Miss Marlow, kinder than I have ever been to you. But I know what I know, and I think I could have stopped you going if I had only reacted swiftly enough. And, no matter what you say, or I try to convince myself to believe, I will always live with the knowledge that you almost died, and I wanted you to!'

The excitement of the day got to her. And by the time Carlo turned up that evening, Cass was lying in bed with her eyes closed and the lights turned down low.

'What happened?' he demanded without any preliminary greeting. In fact, the first Cass knew of his presence was the curt sound of that voice.

She lifted her heavy lids and peered at him. He was out of focus, making the pain behind her eyes throb all the harder. She closed them again, not bothering to reply.

'OK,' he sighed, 'let me guess...' Drawing up a chair, he folded his long body into it. 'The flowers must be from Guido...' She smiled wanly at the accuracy of his guess. The room was heavy with the scent of them. 'A surfeit of emotion from Teresa—my mother informed me of the child's breakdown when she saw you,' he added. 'If it helps any to know this, then I can tell you that it is the first sign of real emotion she has shown since you went overboard.'

'Except when she saw you follow me overboard,' Cass whispered threadily.

'Ah. You have heard of our breakthrough,' he stated with heavy satisfaction.

Cass nodded.

'Ironic, is it not, that she cries for her "daddy" at perhaps the only moment in my life when I cannot respond to it?'

'You've responded since, though, I hope,' Cass murmured wryly.

'Oh, yes—not that it has made much difference to the way she responds to me,' he added grimly. 'She has been barely reachable while you lay so ill. The child bottles too much up.'

'I know,' she whispered.

'You do?' He glanced quizzically at her. 'Then my mother has to have been busy with her tongue,' he decided, shifting things back to his original theme—the one which involved guessing why her temperature had gone sky-high, why her head was throbbing badly, and why the doctor had waylaid him on his way in here to issue a stern lecture on overtiring someone so recently out of a coma! The reason Cass knew all of this was because she had endured the same lecture herself, and been warned that Carlo would be told the selfsame things. 'Yes, I thought so,' he clipped when her mouth twitched appreciatively. 'Is that all?' he enquired drily.

Cass didn't answer. Besides being too weak to do so, she didn't really want to talk about Sabrina's unexpected descent on her.

'No,' he therefore and shrewdly surmised, 'it is not all. Now who have I missed out...?' He sat back, and Cass heard the flimsy hospital chair creak at the same moment he reached out to take hold of her hand. And slowly and at last the pain inside her head began to ease. Why, she refused to analyse, because she knew it had something dangerously to do with his being here with her like this.

'Sabrina,' he said at last. 'It has to have been Sabrina, since I ordered her to come nowhere near you, and she never was a woman to take orders from anyone. Did Sabrina come to spill all her terrible guilts out on your weary shoulders, Cassandra?' he demanded.

'She wanted me to drown out there,' Cass whispered in confirmation.

'Yes,' Carlo sighed, not even trying to deny it.

'But not you.' That much Cass had gleaned for herself from everything everyone had told her.

'No, not me,' he agreed. 'I don't know which horrified her the most—the fact that she did nothing to help you, or my going over the side after you. Whatever,' he dismissed, 'it is all in the past now. You did not drown, neither did I, and Sabrina will have to come to terms with her own conscience, for no one else can do it for her.'

'She's in love with you,' Cass said, forcing her eyes open to look at him. He looked grim and angry, but oh, so wonderful to her hungry senses that she lay there just drinking in the sight of him.

'Sabrina loves Sabrina and the Valenti money,' he brushed off. 'I can forgive her not reacting quickly enough to stop you falling, but I will never forgive her for actually wishing you dead!'

Cass shuddered when he said that. 'You argued with her on the yacht,' she reminded him. 'She was very angry.'

'I told her a few home truths, that was all,' he said dismissively. 'The way she behaved like a vicious little cat towards you all the time was beginning to worry you, Cassandra, so I decided to put a stop to it.'

'She was jealous of me. She saw me as competition.'

'There is no competition,' he clipped. 'Not if it is between a warm and caring woman and a conceited and malicious doll!' His mouth snapped shut, as though he was having difficulty controlling his contempt.

'The way you flirted with her all the time,' Cass accused him hotly, angered by his complete lack of sympathy to someone who must be suffering painfully through his rejection, 'it was only natural that she believed she meant something important to you!'

'Italian men flirt by nature.' He refused to accept responsibility for that attack. 'She knew how innocent it was.'

Did it automatically follow, then, that all the attention he had been paying Cass during her stay here had been a mere nothing? The pain behind her eyes began to throb again, and she shut the sight of him out by closing her eyes.

'She leaves for New York tomorrow,' he went on, 'to make a long stay with some relatives she has there. I think the change will do her good...' And the way he said it made Cass realise that Sabrina had not come out of the ordeal on the yacht much better than Cass herself had. 'And all which remains for you to do is work hard at getting back your strength. Those dark circles around your pretty eyes are not flattering, *caro*, and I wish to see them gone as soon as possible.'

There he goes again, she thought heavily, using the husky intimacy of his voice to charm her with his concern, when he had just admitted himself that there was no real sincerity in it!

'How did you do it?' She changed the subject with the question. 'How did you manage to keep us afloat for so long?'

They were sitting in semi-darkness, and his face was all shadows, but she saw the wry grimace he gave. 'To be truthful, and at the risk of ruining my heroic reputation, I, like you, remember very little. I just—did it,' he said simply. 'It was pure luck that I found you at all...'

'And pure folly to put your own life at risk like that.'

His nod acknowledged it. 'But, on finding you, I only knew that I wasn't about to let either of us go to such a cold and murky death. So...' a short sigh broke from him, as though he, like Cass, had had a surfeit of excitement enough to last a lifetime '...I concentrated on keeping our heads above water.'

'Thank you,' she whispered, bringing his dark eyes up to clash with hers.

His fingers tightened around her own, and Cass felt the life begin to seep back into her, as though a mere touch from him was as good as any tonic a doctor could prescribe.

'Have I at last redeemed myself in your eyes?' he murmured gruffly—no whimsy, but a question asked from the heart that made her own squeeze achingly. 'Can you now bring yourself to forgive me for deserting your sister?'

She looked gravely at him. Accepting that, no matter what else went between them, she at least owed him her assurance that she had forgiven him for the way he'd treated Liz. 'If you say there were—misunderstandings,' she said, 'then I accept your word on that.'

He searched her steady gaze for a long time before nodding briefly in acceptance of what she'd said. Then he was glancing at his watch and sighing softly. 'I have to go,' he murmured. 'The doctor gave me five minutes, and I have been here fifteen.'

He sounded as reluctant to leave her bedside as she was to see him go. And it must have shown on her face because he sent her a rueful smile, then leaned over to press a warm kiss to her cheek before getting to his feet. Then, with that brisk, graceful stride of his, he walked over to the door.

'With any luck,' he said as he reached it, 'they will let me take you home from here in a couple of days. No more visitors, though,' he warned as he glanced back at her. 'My decree, not the doctor's. We won't take the risk on a relapse. Except for myself, of course——' he then smiled disarmingly '—and I shall come and see you to-morrow,' he promised as he opened the door.

'Carlo!' Cass called out quickly before he disappeared. He glanced enquiringly back at her. 'My—my job,' she murmured worriedly. 'Did you manage to save it for me?'

He didn't answer immediately, his gaze fixed thoroughly on her for a moment, then he was striding back to the bed. 'Have you still not learned to trust me, *caro*?' he challenged quietly.

'Of course!' she said, eyes widening in surprise that he even had to ask that question after what they had gone through together. She trusted him with her life! *Had* trusted him with her life.

'Well...' his hands came to rest on the pillows either side of her head, bringing his handsome face close to her own '... did I not ask you to leave your job to me?' When she nodded dumbly, he did too. 'Then why are you worrying about it?'

She laughed, ruefully accepting his arrogant sarcasm. Why was she worrying? Carlo was the kind of man who could charm the birds out of the trees if he wanted to. He would have charmed the powers at be to hold her job for her, she was sure of it.

'I'm not worried,' she assured him smilingly. Yet there was something about the look in his eyes that made her add carefully, 'You do understand about my need of that job, don't you? H-how important it is to me?'

'Oh, I understand, *caro*,' he assured her. 'I understand more than I think you realise.' And he bent to press one last gentle kiss to her lips before going quietly away.

CHAPTER TEN

IT WAS nice to sit out in the warm evening air with the sun just dropping in a big golden ball behind the hills opposite, etching the trees like tall black sentinels against a polished bronze sky.

Cass was alone at last, Terri having been carried complaining to bed by a firm-voiced father informing her that now she had her aunt Cass back, the wonderful days of getting all her own way were over! Terri did not take kindly to this piece of news—nor the further news that Maria would continue to sleep in Cass's bed until her aunt was stronger.

Cass, she had soon found out, had been allocated a different room further down the wing. This one, where she was sitting enjoying the sunset on a terracotta-tiled terrace, feeling rather spoiled and decadent in the spearmint-coloured smooth satin nightdress and matching robe Terri had excitedly presented her with on her return from hospital that afternoon.

She still felt rather shaky on her feet, but otherwise was over her ordeal. The stitches had been removed from her head and the headaches had gone completely. And for the first time in over a week she had been allowed to shampoo her hair, and to feel the silken mass tumbling lightweight and crackling about her shoulders was a sheer relief after the days when it had hung in a limp, lank pelt down her back.

'That child is in need of some firm handling,' Carlo said from just behind her.

Cass turned to smile at him as he came through the open terrace doors. 'You've all been spoiling her,' she scolded. 'She isn't usually so petulant.'

'I accept all blame.' He held up his hands, grimacing as he came to take the soft-cushioned cane chair beside her own, and Cass found herself watching the play of muscle beneath the fine silk covering of his white shirt. Her mouth went dry, and she wanted to look away, but found she couldn't. It was getting worse; ever since their ordeal by sea, she had been tormented constantly with this need to drink him up thirstily all the time.

'She played on your absence and our knowledge that she fretted for you,' he went on grimly. 'To lose you, Cassandra, would be like losing her mother twice over. You must be aware of that.'

'Yes.' Quickly, she looked away from him, her clouded gaze staring out at the glowing sunset.

Coming so close to death had brought home to her more than anything else could have done just how too reliant on her Terri was. If Carlo had not entered the child's orbit, and anything tragic had happened to Cass, then Terri would have been orphaned, with nothing and no one to care what happened to her.

Cass shuddered, knowing from personal experience exactly how that felt.

But Carlo was in her orbit now, she reminded herself bracingly. And he could offer Terri far more love and security than Cass could ever give. His family was large if widely spread, his money enough to ensure the child's future whether he lived to be ninety or died tomorrow— God forbid. Terri was young—young enough to adjust to life without her aunt Cass.

It was time to give her up.

As a trained nanny, Cass had been warned about this moment, and what a wrench it could be, but, as an aunt who had loved and cared for her niece as if she were her own child, it would be a whole lot more than that. As Teresa was the only family she had left in the world, it was going to be sheer anguish.

But do it she must. And she would become what she should have been to Terri from the beginning—a visiting aunt who moved briefly in and out of her life. The kind of aunt who showered gifts on her niece, and spoiled her to death when she was around—which would not be often, she added with a sad little twist to her mouth. Because the other reason she must leave here quickly and keep her visits sparse and brief was sitting beside her right now.

'Stop thinking!' The harsh cut of Carlo's voice brought her head swinging around to find him sitting with his dark face drawn into taut lines of anger.

'I'm sorry?' she said, surprised by his grating attack.

His eyes were fierce on her, the anger seeming to come from somewhere far deeper within him than a mere irritation at her long silence.

'I can see the little cogs turning in your brain!' he growled, jerking suddenly to his feet to stride over to the white-painted rail hung heavy with clambering vines. He spun back to face her. 'I could see you considering options and drawing conclusions without bothering to consult anyone else!' He gave an impatient sigh when she continued to stare at him blankly. 'Have you ever relied on anyone else to help make decisions with you?'

'I—well, no,' she admitted, too disconcerted by his unexpected attack to be anything but honest.

Her early years living the institutional life in a state orphanage did not lend themselves to sharing childish little problems. And later, when she had been farmed out into various foster-homes, she found she couldn't confide easily, had lost the ability to share problems. So, for as far back into her life as she could remember, Cass had been making her own decisions, thinking the problems through carefully before drawing conclusions.

She looked at Carlo, and took in a deep breath. 'We have to talk about Teresa, Carlo,' she ventured tentatively. 'It really can't be put off any longer.'

'Can't it?' He sounded so unapproachable that she had to brace herself to continue.

'You must agree with me by now that she has to live here with you.'

'Have I ever suggested differently?' he drawled.

'No!' she sighed, wishing she could make out his features in the growing gloom, but he was too far away, standing there with his lean profile turned on her, his tense figure almost merging with the tall, straight fir trees lining the hillside behind him.

'She needs you, Carlo,' she pushed on stubbornly. 'She's already mounted the biggest hurdle by accepting you for what you are to her at last. The rest should come easier. And I am confident that she can learn—with yours and your mother's and even Maria's help—to do without me now.'

'Except that she doesn't need to be put through the anguish of "doing without you",' he mocked her grimly. 'Not when there is another alternative open to us—and you know it.'

'No.' He didn't need to explain further for her to know what he meant; the sudden rush of heat to her senses did it for him. But that was one solution she was determined to refuse—and keep on refusing until Carlo gave up on it. 'No,' she said again, and more firmly. 'I have my own life to lead. And I won't be—coerced into sacrificing all of it to Teresa when I know she will be just as loved and cared for without me—if not more so.' She released a sigh, her fingers curling tightly together on her lap because each word she said was increasing the weight of loneliness she was already beginning to feel.

'I have a good job to go home to,' she went on bravely, 'and the chance of getting some kind of order into my own life which I——'

'No, you don't,' Carlo put in quietly.

'What?' she frowned, not understanding what he meant.

'You don't have a job to go home to England to,' he said.

Cass blinked in confusion. 'But y-you told me you would see to it!' she whispered. 'Y-you insisted I should leave everything to you!'

'And I did see to it,' he told her. 'I tendered your resignation for you.'

Silence fell like a stone while she sat there just staring at him. Then she shook her head. 'I don't believe you,' she said at last. 'You asked me to trust you. And I know you wouldn't go back on your word,' she stated positively.

A strange smile twisted Carlo's mouth, one which suggested that she had managed to pierce through his thick hide to the heart of the man for once. 'I'm sorry, Cassandra,' he said quietly, 'but I tendered your resignation formally and in writing the day after you awoke at the hospital. The school's acceptance of it arrived on my desk this morning.'

'No!' she cried, coming jerkily to her feet.

The sudden movement was too much for her weakened limbs, and they wobbled beneath her, sending her hand reaching out to steady herself on the chair-back. It began to slide on the terracotta floor, the cane legs screeching piercingly in the quietness of the evening.

'A habit of yours, grabbing hold of the wrong safety-line, isn't it, *caro*?' he mocked as his hands came firm around her waist, drawing her against him. 'When are you going to admit that you are being held in the safest place you can be right now?'

'But—why?' she choked, pulling right away from him to stand trembling in hurt bewilderment. 'How could you do it?'

'You know why,' he sighed, then snapped out impatiently, 'You owe me, Cassandra—you owe Teresa. I did warn you over a week ago that I would not let you simply walk away from us as if neither of us mattered to you!'

'This isn't fair!' she protested, feeling wretched because he was giving her enough excuses to give in to him, more than enough to salve her own pride if she did. 'You're pushing me into a corner I don't deserve to be pushed into! You don't have to go as far as marrying me to make Terri accept you—she already has!'

'Sit down again, *mi amante*—you're trembling,' he advised.

And she was, trembling so badly that her legs were threatening to give way beneath her. But for some reason that only helped to infuriate her all the more.

'No, I won't sit down!' she snapped out angrily. 'You have no right—no right to take over my life for me!'

'And you have no right to be even considering deserting Teresa!' he threw right back.

They glared at each other across the half-yard width separating them. It was a stalemate, and Cass groaned wretchedly in the knowledge of it.

'Look...' Carlo sighed, obviously seeing something in her face that told him she couldn't take much more of this tonight '...you're tired, and this is far too soon to be having this kind of discussion. It will keep for another time.'

'What other time?' she whispered bitterly. 'Every time I try to state my opinion, you start bullying me!'

His laugh was short and rueful. 'With a stubborn woman like you, Cassandra, you need bullying. Look at you,' he added on a sigh, coming to take hold of her by the shoulders, 'you are so tired you can barely cope. Yet still you stand here fighting me.' He pulled her close, his hand burrowing into her hair so that he could push her face into his warm, muscled shoulder.

'You have to see that marriage isn't the answer, Carlo,' she pleaded with him, too weak to move away from him, and despising herself for staying in his arms.

'It is the only answer, *mi amore*,' he insisted, his mouth warm against her cheek. 'We have a great many things going for us if you would only let yourself consider them.'

Have we? she wondered bleakly. Then sighed into his shoulder because standing so close to him like this felt so wonderful that she never wanted to move again.

'Come on,' he said, shifting his arm so that it became supportive around her waist. 'It is time you were in bed.'

She let him hold her close as he guided her inside, where a single soft lamp illuminated the bed. He pulled back the sheets and sat her down, and, exhausted, she let him remove her slippers and her robe, and she even let him slide her gently into the bed and pull the covers up over her.

His hand came up to stroke her hair on to the cool white pillow, dark eyes so tender on her that she wanted to weep. Then his mouth came gently on to hers, replaying that other gentle kiss which had first ignited this throb of feeling between them: passive, caring and seeming to invite their spirits to touch. She didn't try to pull away, she didn't even want to. And this, she acknowledged sadly, was her biggest weakness—her need for kisses like this...

He was smiling when he eventually lifted his head. 'Goodnight, Cassandra,' he murmured, and bent to touch his mouth to her own again before quietly going away.

Cass stared after him through dull eyes. She was going to have to steal away like a thief if she was ever to have a chance of getting away from him. Because Carlo Valenti only had to touch her and she was lost, her desire for him overriding everything else.

He paused by the door, turning back to smile at her in a way that made her senses flip, and she had to bite down hard on her bottom lip to stop herself from begging him to come back, join her here in this big lonely bed.

Just one night . . . she thought enticingly. Would it be too much to ask, just one beautiful spirit-touching night in his arms to take away with me when I do go?

The door closed behind him, and suddenly she was alone, the opportunity gone with him. Shivering, she turned on to her side, telling herself that it was for the best. Her leaving here as soon as she could get away was for the best. Best for everyone. Carlo, Terri and most importantly herself.

But she wished the future didn't yawn so wide and bleak in front of her without them. She wished she at least had a job to lose herself in.

A single tear trickled down her cheek and lay there untouched, to dry on its own, the heaviness of depression and the need to sleep dragging her downwards.

She wished she hadn't fallen in love with Carlo Valenti.

She wished her sister had never so much as set eyes on him.

She wished she didn't have to leave this place . . .

She dreamt she was drowning that night. Experiencing once again the horror of plunging down into the murky depths of a cold, dark sea.

Only this time she couldn't fight her way back to the surface again, and the air began to burn in her lungs while her body was cold, freezing cold, being dragged deeper and deeper despite the desperate thrashing of her arms and legs to halt the terrifying pull.

'No!' she screamed inside her head. 'I don't want to——'

'Cassandra!'

Strong arms wrapped themselves around her, pulling her upwards. And she began sobbing with relief.

'Cassandra...' It was Carlo. Of course it was Carlo! He had come to save her again. 'Wake up; you are having a bad dream...'

She came battling back through the murky wash of sleep to find herself cradled against his warm chest.

'It was awful!' she whispered raggedly, the repercussions of the nightmare still shuddering through her. 'I couldn't stop sinking. And it was so cold!' She shivered, buried her face in the warmth of his throat, so glad he was there that she clutched at him.

'And no wonder!' he rasped, pushing the damp tendrils of hair away from her icy face. 'It's freezing in here!' She sensed him glancing around the bedroom, then a harsh sigh shook his chest. 'The terrace doors are still wide open. And the wind has changed direction and is blowing right into this room. It is no wonder you dreamt you were cold!'

And it was only then that Cass realised that not only was she shivering, but her teeth were actually chattering with the cold, her hands like ice where they clutched at him.

'Come on.' Giving her no chance to argue, Carlo stood up with her in his arms. 'There is no way you can sleep in here tonight—*Dio*,' he muttered angrily, 'you could have developed a second dose of pneumonia in here, and it would have been all my fault! I forgot to close those damned doors!'

'You weren't to know the wind would turn around,' she defended him. 'Where did you come from?' She lifted her head to level questioning eyes on him. 'Was I shouting so loud that you could hear me all the way down the...?' Her voice trailed away, her eyes already noticing the spill of light coming from an open door across the room she hadn't previously noticed.

'This room joins with mine,' he explained. 'Your cries filtered through the connecting door. You can finish the night in my bed,' he informed her as he carried her into his bedroom. 'I shall find another bed to sleep in.' He placed her down among the rumpled covers, still deliciously warm and scented from his own body. 'Is there anything I can get you?' he enquired as he tried to disentangle himself from her clutching arms. 'A warm drink, or...?'

'Don't go,' she begged, holding tightly on to him.

He went still, gazing into her huge, luminous green eyes where the horrors of her bad dream still lurked.

'Please...' she whispered, knowing what she was tempting him with, and not caring. She needed him with her. Needed to feel the comforting strength of his arms around her. 'I don't w-want to be alone.'

'*Caro,*' he sighed, shaking his dark head, 'you are playing with fire, asking this of me.'

Small white teeth bit down on her full and trembling bottom lip, but her eyes still pleaded with him.

He gave a pained groan. 'If I come into that bed with you, Cassandra, I shall make love to you,' he warned, seeming to need to spell it out to her, as if his own conscience demanded it of him. 'For I cannot lie beside you and not do so; you do know that, don't you?'

'Yes,' she breathed, already beginning to feel the exquisite torment of her own desire snaking sensually through her.

She sensed his uncertainty, saw his dark eyes flicker, his mouth quiver, that square, sculptured jaw clench as he waged an uneven battle with himself. Her fingers stretched then curled into the warm skin at his nape, her breasts lifting and falling on a silken sigh. And he uttered a hoarse groan, and brought his mouth down hungrily on to her own.

Something had happened during her second battle with the sea. As though the dream had given her a fierce awareness of her own entity, and she needed this, him, to give her life some purpose.

Her life to date had been stuffed full of so many other things that she had never had time for men or lovers. Her ideas on making love were hazy at most. Mere technical details gleaned from what she'd read or heard. But suddenly she was desperate to find out for herself what it was like to give oneself entirely to another person, to join, on the physical as well as spiritual plane. Know the power of a man's possession.

And, as if he seemed to know all of this intuitively, Carlo did not simply throw off their clothes and overwhelm her with his body. In fact, he barely touched her at all unless it was where his hungry lips caressed. He leaned above her, her hands locked around his neck while he braced himself with his hands placed either side of her body, and began to kiss her, slowly, sensually, on her mouth, her eyes, her soft cheeks, then back to her mouth again, drawing her through a slow build-up of pleasure that had her pulses deepening at the sweet, sweet torment of feeling he was inciting inside her, until she could bear it no more, and urged him closer to her with the trembling pull of her hands.

He began to caress her then, using his fingers to follow the rounded shape of her slender body. His thumb probed the thrusting points of her nipples beneath the fine silk covering of her nightdress, and a fierce sting of pleasure shot through her, bringing her body arching up to meet the caress, and he pushed the silk aside to expose the fullness of her breasts so that his mouth could take the place of his thumbs.

Her nightdress slipped away by slow degrees, urged by the warm brush of his hands followed by the sensual lick of his tongue, until she was writhing beneath him, so alive to his touch that she became lost to it, eyes closed, the air whispering shallowly from her lungs, burning in the hot tide of deep, throbbing pleasure.

She barely noticed his own growing desire, the harsh rush of his breath or the tight clenching of his body as he continued to hold himself above her. And if she had opened her eyes she would probably have cried out in fear of the passionate intensity written on his face. But she heard the husky murmur of his voice, seducing her, making love to her with the luxurious words of his native tongue, urging her onwards without her actually realising it, encouraging, lifting her.

He came to lie beside her, naked and hot, his skin like finely stretched leather to her exploring lips, moist and tasting slightly of salt, and she sucked greedily at it, her fingers drawing through the thick mat of hair at his chest, loving the ripple of hard muscle, the broken gasps she could urge from him.

When he parted her thighs with the gentle pressure of his hand, she fell back against the bed, held breathless by the depth of sensation his touch drew from her.

'No,' she groaned, frightened and disturbed by this new wave of pure electric feeling.

'Easy, *amore*,' he murmured soothingly. 'Don't fight it. Let it flow...'

Let it flow... The words played over and over in her mind as her body quickened, the air leaving her in soft, soulful little sighs, and her limbs became leaden, filled with a hot, sweet, tingling liquid which held her in its exquisite thrall.

'Carlo,' she whispered breathlessly.

It was then that he came over her, sliding between her thighs, and slowly, with his body held taut in an effort to control his own needs, he thrust inside her. Explosions went off in her head, the moment's pain making her arch in groaning protest beneath him while his hands held her face still so that he could ravish her mouth with a kiss so intense that she could do no other than submit to him.

Then she felt herself relaxing, the pain swept away on a tidal wave of feeling which had her moving restlessly beneath him, her fingers sliding on the slick skin of his shoulders as he began to move, slowly at first, then deeper, and as she cried out his name in frantic delirium he began moving faster until they both went toppling over the edge into a world she had never visited before, nor wanted to leave again . . .

CHAPTER ELEVEN

CASS came awake to a wonderful feeling of inner peace which had her body stretching languidly in the bed and a soft sigh of pleasure escaping her lips—before she remembered, and went perfectly still, not even breathing as her mind played back tormenting images of her own sensual wantonness of the night before.

What had she done? Her eyes flicked open, staring in horror at the ceiling above her head, terrified to move a single muscle in case she awoke the man beside her.

Only, she realised with a start, there was no man beside her!

Blinking, trying to make some sense out of the hectic muddle her brain was in, she sat up, pushing the tumbled fall of her hair away from her face to find herself in her own room, her own bed, with the gentle morning breeze disturbing the soft drapes around the open french windows.

Had she dreamt it all? Her cheeks began to burn, hot embarrassment curling its way through her, and she placed a trembling hand over her heart in an effort to stop it thumping—only to gasp and glance down at where her hand lay over one smooth and very naked breast.

My God, she thought, not a dream! And even as she struggled to accept what she had actually allowed to happen last night, her flesh began to tingle in memory of his caresses, the muscles deep down inside her body curling in pleasurable acknowledgement of his passionate possession.

Please, God, she pleaded desperately, closing her eyes to send up her useless prayer, tell me I didn't throw myself at him last night!

The bedroom door-handle rattled, and she made a quick grab at the sheet to tug it over her guilty nakedness. Cheeks glowing red, her eyes dark green and haunted, she waited for him to enter the room, face her with what they had done...

Terri's little face peeped around the door, and she almost fainted with relief. 'Cass!' She bounced into the room. 'You're awake at last! I thought you were going to sleep all day!' The little girl ran to the bed and jumped on to it, reaching out with her arms to give Cass a hug and a good morning kiss, then she sat back on her heels to beam her a delighted smile. 'My daddy says we can stay here for ever and ever!' she announced, her face suffused with a too long suppressed excitement. 'He says you're going to get married, and I can be bridesmaid and wear a pretty frock, and...'

Cass shut her eyes, refusing to believe any of this was happening. She was still asleep, she decided. She had to be. She didn't have that awful nightmare last night. Carlo hadn't come and gathered her into his arms, taken her to his bed, laid her down, made beautiful love to her. And Teresa was not sitting here, beaming at her, telling her she and Carlo were——

'I thought you were told not to awaken your aunt,' a voice scolded from the doorway.

Cass's eyes flew open; dark and defensive, they stared across the room to where Mrs Valenti stood, leaning heavily on her two sticks, smiling at the pair of them.

'I didn't,' the child protested, 'did I, Cass? She was already awake,' she insisted, when Cass made no reply. 'I was just telling her that I'm going to be a bridesmaid when she marries my daddy, and——'

'Chattering her into exhaustion before she has even had her breakfast,' Teresa's grandmother inserted drily. 'How are you this morning, Cassandra?' Those warm brown eyes so like Carlo's and Teresa's turned on to Cass.

'I...' Her tongue cleaved itself to the roof of her mouth, and she had to swallow tensely to be able to speak at all.

'Teresa...' Mrs Valenti came slowly forwards '...go and tell Maria that your aunt is awake and ready for breakfast.'

'OK.' The child beamed at them both, reached over to give Cass another hug, then scrambled off the bed, only to pause and turn back, her big eyes shining with untethered happiness. 'Everything is going to be perfect now, isn't it, Cass?' she sighed out rapturously. 'We don't have to go back to Fulham. We don't have to go anywhere now my daddy is going to look after us!' Then she turned and skipped out of the room, thankfully not seeming to require any reply.

They both watched her go, her steps so light she was almost floating. Then Mrs Valenti turned to leave Cass with a rueful look. 'She has been like that ever since Carlo announced your plans this morning.'

'Mrs Valenti——' Cass tried to get a hold on herself '—I...'

'You must call me Mamma now, my dear,' she was ordered, then the old lady let out a sigh and lowered herself into the chair beside Cass's bed. 'I am so pleased for you both. And I have not seen my son looking so happy in many a long year—thank you for that, Cassandra,' she said sincerely.

God in heaven, Cass thought frantically, this thing is literally galloping away from me! 'Where is Carlo, Mrs—M-mamma?' she corrected awkwardly. 'I must speak to him.'

The old lady shook her head. 'I am sorry, but he is not here. He received an urgent call this morning, and has had to fly out to Rome.'

Rome? He sets this place by its ears by making an announcement like that, then casually flies off to Rome?

'He expects to be gone about three days,' his mother informed her. 'There's an irritating problem with one of his managers who has taken ill. He would have explained this to you himself, of course, only you were still sleeping like a baby when he received the call, so he just carried you back to your own room, and decided to let you rest...'

The heat of embarrassment flooded Cass's face again, and she just sat there staring at the older lady while the latter stared right back, her eyes saying what her words had not, and that was that, as far as anyone here was concerned, she and Carlo were effectively married already.

On a groan of defeat, Cass sank back against the pillows, and closed her eyes.

'Do not be embarrassed, Cassandra,' his mother soothed. 'I am a sophisticated woman of the world after all. Not always tied to this valley by my walking sticks,' she added ruefully. 'And I was well aware that you and my son have been moving towards a closer relationship ever since you arrived here. The fact that you have— pre-empted your marriage vows is not something I condone, of course, but I do understand both your feelings, especially after that terrible ordeal where you almost lost each other...'

'I have to speak to him,' Cass whispered thickly, feeling an intolerable pressure begin to build in her chest.

'And you shall,' his mother assured, 'just as soon as he—ah.' The distinctive sound of rattling china put a stop on their conversation. And Cass stared through what seemed a long, dark tunnel of shock at Teresa, skipping happily along beside Maria, as they came into the room with her breakfast.

Breakfast, lunch, dinner, and breakfast a second time, and still Cass had not been given the opportunity to speak to the man who had placed her in this mess. And in the end the full three days went by without her hearing a single word from him. Three days that were filled with the ever-tightening coil of Carlo's arrogant announcement as his mother threw them all into a bewildering whirl of activity in the form of wedding plans. Invitations to write out. Dresses to choose and have made. Flowers to decide upon. Music—church music, reception music—'The valley will be ringing in celebration two weeks from now!' she laughed. And Cass wanted to hit someone, Carlo Valenti preferably, if the conniving devil hadn't effectively disappeared off the face of the earth!

Her emotions became raw, her nerves ragged. She jumped when anyone so much as spoke to her, and continually had to bite down hard on her tongue to stop herself screaming in hysterical protest. She couldn't sleep, but spent the next two nights tossing in her bed in restless torment, and when she did eventually fall into an exhausted slumber it was only to be visited by a tall, dark man who set her senses pounding with the magical touch of his hands.

He arrived back mid-afternoon of the third day. Cass watched dully the sun bounce off the white Ferrari as it snaked its way down the side of the valley. She was sitting in the clearing on the hill behind the house, having escaped the mad preparations before she did actually give in and start screaming.

She didn't make any attempt to go down and meet him, but just sat there, picking absently at the short dry grass with her fingers, her chin resting on her up-drawn knees, eyes following the Ferrari's passage into the valley and across the little bridge until it became blocked from view by the house.

A few minutes went by before she saw him appear again, striding around the side of the house to pause by the wall which kept the horses contained in their pasture. He was wearing a white shirt, his powerful legs encased in dark cloth.

A buzz of awareness began to hum inside her, centring itself in the low pit of her stomach, from where it sent shock waves rippling out to every part of her. She watched him turn in a slow, searching circle, waited for his gaze to come her way. She was wearing a simple beige cotton skirt and a coffee-coloured blouse. Nothing remarkable, but she knew, without her having to do a single thing, that he would find her. It was as if there was a telepathic homing device set between the two of them.

He did, and for a long moment he just stood there gazing up through the long terraces of fruit trees, the jet-black smoothness of his hair gleaming in the afternoon sun. Then he moved, began striding down the path which would bring him to her, and Cass allowed herself a small sigh while she waited for him to climb the hill to where she was.

'You look like a poor trapped deer, sitting there,' his voice drawled lazily from behind her. 'Viewing your fenced-in territory from its most unequivocal point.'

'Hog-tied and tethered is the most appropriate phrase which comes to mind,' she threw back dully.

He laughed softly, and walked forwards to drop down on the grass beside her. She was instantly made aware of him, of his long, lean powerful body just an inch away from her own, the clean scent of him, his dark good looks, and now his potent sexuality. Her heart fluttered in her breast, and she set her teeth together behind her lips.

'Why did you do it?'

'Make love to you?' he deliberately misunderstood. 'You all but begged me to, *caro*. I am man enough to be swayed by such—enchanting persuasion.'

The colour crept up her cheeks, the guilty mark of truth. She didn't look at him—hadn't done so since he appeared in the clearing—but she could feel his gaze fixed intently on her, knew he was as alive to the feelings buzzing between them as she was.

Her eyes blurred with tears—why, she wasn't sure, but something desperate was weeping inside her heart. He reached up to gently brush her hair away from the side of her face, his fingertips lingering on her soft, warm cheek.

'You were innocent, *mi amante*,' he murmured huskily, 'and yet you gave that innocence to me with such sweet, sweet passion. Will it hurt you so much to give the rest of yourself to me?'

'T-to you I'm just a means to a neat and tidy end!' She turned to look at him, the torment in her eyes deepening at the sheer nerve-wrenching beauty of him. 'What happens when you really fall in love with someone?' she whispered bleakly. 'Where do we go then?'

His eyes were grave on her anxious face. 'If anyone is likely to fall in love, *caro*, then it will be you, not me.' On a restless jerk, he plucked a dry stem of grass from its root, sighing as he leaned forwards to rest his forearms on his bent knees. 'You are young and beautiful, enchanting to be with. Have you no idea how rare you are—twenty-five years old and never been touched?' he muttered, giving an impatient shake of his sleek, dark head. 'Barely kissed from what I have discovered about you!' he tagged on harshly. His eyes flashed her a condemning look, and Cass looked away, hurt by what she heard as his mockery.

'I can't marry you, Carlo,' she told him.

'And why not?' he demanded. 'If you honestly believe, Cassandra, that after making love to you I will let you just walk away from me, then you can think again!'

'But I don't love you!' she cried, biting hard on her trembling bottom lip because that lie had rent at her soul.

His head shot around, eyes so black that she felt as though she could drown in them. 'You love Teresa—why can't you love her father also?'

'Liz!' she cried out wretchedly.

'Ah, yes, your poor lost sister and the mother of my child,' he drawled. 'I wondered when we should get to her. What do you want to know, *caro*?' he questioned bitterly. 'Whether she lost her heart to her Italian lover only to have it thrown right back when he had finished with it?' She flinched at his cynicism, and Carlo let out a short, hard laugh. 'Perhaps, Cassandra, it may please you to know that you are not the first Marlow I have offered marriage to.'

No, it didn't please her. It hurt like hell. Was that all she was to him, an acceptable substitute for her dead sister? 'You were in love with her,' she breathed, wondering painfully if she was destined always to have her own identity lost in the intricate tangle of her sister's life.

'Love? No.' He shook his head. 'I—admired her. Desired her. But love never came into what Elizabeth and I shared during those few short weeks we were together.' He grimaced, showing by his expression that he did not like what that confession made him.

Neither did Cass, and she went to get up, not wanting to just sit here quietly beside him while he thoroughly shattered her every illusion. But Carlo stopped her by reaching out to grasp her wrist, firmly anchoring her back on the hard, tufted grass.

'Stay,' he instructed. 'The truth must come out if we are ever to move forwards in our relationship.'

What relationship? One where she played substitute to Liz with both her child and her lover? Bitterness welled up inside Cass, all the more acid because it was aimed almost exclusively at a sister whom she had always loved so unreservedly.

'When Elizabeth and I came together as lovers here in San Remo, we both did so with the understanding that we would part when the promotion she was working on for my motels was finished,' he told Cass frankly. 'Neither she nor I wanted any emotional entanglements. I was still recovering from the loss of my wife and son, and she enjoyed the freedom both her career and her single status offered her too much to want to give it up.'

Of course, Cass had suspected Liz wasn't celibate exactly. She had been a mature and very sophisticated woman. And beautiful—too beautiful not to have had some love-affairs in her life. But could she have been as life-hardened as Carlo was making her out to be?

'We parted as friends,' he went on, 'and with no plans to come together again in some other time or place.'

'Like take like,' she compared bitterly, then shook her head, lowering it so that her hair fell like a glistening curtain to hide the distaste written on her face.

Carlo just shrugged. 'Yes, I suppose you could call it that—not a nice view for someone with your own high moral principles, I acknowledge,' he admitted, 'but the truth, even though it casts both myself and your sister in a poor light.'

Above them the sky was a pure azure blue, all around them the tangy scent of citrus filled the air, birds were trilling out their perpetual melodies, and the odd buzz of a bee sawed lazily by. The valley spread out like a lush green paradise all around them, and Cass felt like weeping.

'She went back to London,' he continued flatly, his fingers absently smoothing across the satin skin of her wrist, setting the pulse there racing, 'and we had no contact at all for the next two months. Then a mutual friend of ours—another model,' he explained, 'called me to tell me Elizabeth was pregnant with my child.'

'So you wrote to her and advised her to get an abortion.'

'No.' He turned to glare at her. 'You are always—*always* jumping to the worst conclusions about me!' he said harshly. 'Why has it not hit you yet that it was Elizabeth who wanted that abortion?'

'Because Terri is here to prove otherwise!' she cried.

Carlo nodded. 'And my opinion of your sister lifted out from the gutter it had sunk into the moment I found out she had not actually carried out what she had told me she had already done!'

'Oh, I see,' she drawled, 'so it's all Liz's fault, and you didn't provide that fat cheque along with a letter warning her never to contact you again!' She snatched her wrist away from him, and he sighed impatiently as he watched the way she rubbed angrily where his fingers had just caressed.

'Listen to me, you aggravating little witch!' he bit out suddenly, moving so quickly that she didn't have time to defend herself as he came over her, sending her falling back against the grass with his hard body pinning her there. '*Dio*, Cassandra, I had already lost one son,' he reminded her rawly. 'Do you honestly think I am so heartless that I could condone the loss of another child?'

'Oh, God,' she choked, hating herself for forcing him to have to say that. She knew he was telling her the truth. It was just her own reluctance to listen which made her hit out at him.

'I flew out immediately to London with the express purpose of asking her to marry me! Don't misunder-

stand me,' he put in grimly, 'I was no more in love with
your sister than she was with me, but I did see where
my duty lay, and it was with the mother of my future
child!' he rasped. 'In the end, my—grand gesture meant
nothing. Elizabeth was appalled to see me. No,' he muttered then, shaking his head on the bitter memories of
five years ago, 'she was more than that. She was terrified. She had already made arrangements for an
abortion, and she was frightened I was going to make
her change her mind. We argued——' he grimaced
'—but slowly I began to reach her conscience, and in
the end she reluctantly agreed to keep the child and marry
me.'

'You bullied her, you mean,' Cass accused.

'Yes,' he sighed. 'I bullied her. I spent the next few
days in London making arrangements for our marriage,
then had to fly back here to clear up some urgent business
I had left pending. A few days later,' he went on hoarsely,
'I received a letter from her telling me she had changed
her mind, and that it was no use me trying to do anything about it because she had already had an abortion.'

Cass stiffened beneath him. 'But why should she tell
you that when it was so patently untrue?' she demanded.

'Still doubting my word, *caro*?' he drawled cynically.

'No,' she sighed. 'Just trying to understand, because
it doesn't make any sense for her to lie to you like that.'

'I still have the letter if you wish to see it,' he said,
and sat up and away from her, his movements tense and
bitter. 'Though I have to warn you that it does not make
pleasant reading. She had, apparently, won a fantastic
two-year contract advertising Pierre LeMonde's latest
perfume and body-care range. It meant world-wide TV
coverage and all the glitter that went along with it.'

Cass sat up too. 'Which does not explain why she told
you she had terminated her pregnancy when it wasn't
true.'

'Yes, it does,' Carlo contradicted. 'You said it yourself a moment ago, *caro*—I am a bully.' He grimaced on the confession. 'Your sister told me that lie because she did not want me racing back to London to stop her—which I would have done,' he acknowledged. 'Even if it had meant by taking her to court to do it, I would have stopped her from killing our child. But even I had no choice but to accept a *fait accompli*,' he pointed out. 'I can only assume,' he went on after a heavy moment, 'that, when it came to it, Elizabeth found she could not go through with her plan. But, by then hurt and angry enough to want to kill her, I took my revenge by sending her that cheque—for services rendered was its implication,' he admitted heavily. 'And, as you know, I did not hold buck on the insults in the accompanying letter. Elizabeth must have decided that a man who could write such ugly words was not fit to be a father at all, and so became determined not to tell me of her change of heart.'

He was being very kind, sharing half the blame with Elizabeth, but really Cass was aware of how unfair her sister had been in not telling him the truth when she must have known how much Carlo had wanted Teresa.

'All in all,' Cass sighed, 'we Marlows have not been very kind to you, have we?'

'*You* have,' he argued gruffly. 'You have been more than kind, more than fair. Without knowing the reasons for my sending Elizabeth that cheque and letter, you were prepared to give me a chance to prove myself a fit father for Teresa. Your open mind and fresh, clean honesty has made me admire you. And,' he added quietly, 'it has also taught me to forgive Elizabeth for keeping Teresa from me all these years.'

Carlo reached for her then, turning her body into his. 'I love you,' he murmured huskily, and brought his mouth down on to hers, kissing her with a gentle urgency which slowly gained a response from her. Her

fingers tangled in his hair, her body beginning to pulse
to a rhythm he personally set, and she sighed softly in
weak surrender.

Almost immediately they were lost in each other,
straining against the frustrating barrier of clothes,
wanting to join, be one, immerse themselves in the hot
flare of ungoverned passion.

'How could you leave me alone to face all those
knowing faces the other morning?' she flared at him right
out of the blaze of passion.

Rueful at her sudden outburst, Carlo grinned, and
suddenly he was all lazy macho arrogance and lethal
Italian charm, pushing her back against the dry, springy
turf so that his body could press provocatively against
her own.

'The emergency was real,' he defended himself, 'and,
as we were both asleep when Maria brought the message
to me, what did you expect me to do—pretend I had no
idea how you happened to be in my bed instead of your
own?' He gave a typically Latin shrug.

'And the marriage bit?' she demanded, giving an in-
voluntary gasp as he moved against her, his thighs
thrusting enticingly against the sensitive hollow of her
own. 'How do you explain that away?'

'Easily,' he said, exciting her with the teasing light in
his eyes. 'The one thing automatically pre-empts the
other. We were caught red-handed, *mi amore*,' he murmured drily. 'Though next time I make love to you, I
shall ensure beforehand that we cannot be disturbed.'

'Who said there was going to be a next time?' She put
up this one last stand of defiance against his overbearing
confidence.

'I could take you now, and the only cries you would
make would be those of exquisite pleasure,' he derided
her challenge. 'You have no idea, *mi amore*,' he then
added gruffly, 'how frighteningly passionate you are.'

'Well,' she gasped as his mouth came to taste her arching throat, 'I won't be labelled any man's mistress, that's for sure.'

'You will never be anyone's mistress but mine!' he decreed, and smothered any more arguments she might have with his mouth.

As the passion in the kiss deepened, she curved closer to him, her arms winding around his shoulders to hold him close, gasping as the cold rush of air to her breasts told her he had freed them from their lacy cups, hearing his low groan of pleasure with a heightening of her own desire, feeling the throbbing push of his arousal when his hand curved her hips to press her against him.

'It is time, *amore*,' he murmured against her hungry mouth, 'to murmur those sweet little words which sent me spinning over the edge the last time I held you like this.'

She smiled, knowing exactly what he was referring to. It was one of those memories from the other night which had horrified her the most, and had kept her in a state of high tension ever since, waiting for him to come back and taunt her with them.

'I love you,' she whispered, the relief in actually confessing it bringing the tears flooding into her eyes. 'I do so love you, Carlo.'

His kiss spiralled them away again while the mountainside soothed them with its sun-drenched sense of peace. His shirt came apart in her impatient hands, and, on a satisfied sigh, she pressed her breasts against the hard warmth of him, smiling when he shuddered in response.

'We cannot make love here,' he groaned out painfully, lowering his dark head to the sweet-scented hollow between her breasts, 'not in full view of the whole valley!'

'Then take me back to the house,' she urged, revelling in the sweet taste of his muscled shoulder.

'I can't make love to you there, either, dammit!' he sighed, sucking in a deep breath of air before sliding off her. 'My mother has banned our sharing a bed until after our wedding,' he informed her drily, and Cass closed her eyes in pained chagrin.

He turned his head to look at her, 'All right, *caro*?' he murmured gently. 'It is going to be difficult, I know. But I think my mother is right that we should wait until we have given our full commitment to each other.'

'And to think——' Cass managed to find a light note among the emotions pummelling inside her '—I wanted to hit you for arrogantly arranging our marriage to take place in two short weeks!' She rolled on to her stomach to lean over him, her green eyes rueful.

Carlo smiled, and threaded his fingers into her free-flowing hair. 'So, you will marry me?' he questioned. 'I am half out of my mind with need for you, *amante*,' he went on huskily before she had a chance to say a word. 'But I do not want to push you into something you are not yet ready for.'

'Of course I want to marry you,' she assured him, her expression softening into gentle love.

'You refused me the night you had your nightmare,' he reminded her grimly.

'I refused to marry a man who didn't love me,' she corrected, then smiled a little wanly. 'I thought you were asking me for Terri's sake. And it just wasn't enough for me. I wanted all of you or nothing—selfish and greedy though it sounds.'

'So you offered me the gift of your precious innocence with the intention, I think, of leaving this valley for good.'

She nodded. 'I wanted that one night in your arms to take with me when I left here,' she confessed. 'It didn't seem too much to take at the time, but...' A soft sigh whispered from her.

'But one night was not enough, was it?' he concluded for her. 'Even without Maria finding us in bed and giving me the excuse to force your hand, you could not have gone away.'

'I woke up wanting you.'

'And I you.' He drew her down against him, his mouth brushing against her hair. 'I lied to you before when I told you Maria found us sleeping,' he told her. 'She found me wide awake just watching you sleep. I had plenty of time to carry you back to your own bed so nobody would have been any the wiser about how we spent our night. But I had already decided, you see, that I wanted her to find you there, wanted the excuse to trap you.'

'You actually planned my embarrassment?' Cass gasped.

'I am in love with you,' Carlo excused his methods. 'It was a God-given opportunity to tie you to me, and I was going to take it, no matter how angry it made you.'

'Then you ran away and left me to face them all alone!' she exclaimed, accusing him of cowardice.

'I ran away and left *Teresa* to face you with it,' he amended, smiling unrepentantly. 'I knew you would not have the cold-hearted cruelty to take away the child's happiness at our news—no matter how much it made you hate me.'

'But I don't hate you. I love you,' she reminded him softly, and lowered her mouth on to his.

HARLEQUIN CELEBRATES
THE SEASON OF SHARING
AND FAMILY WITH

Friends, Families, Lovers

Harlequin introduces the latest member in its family of
seasonal collections. Following in the footsteps of the popular
My Valentine, *Just Married* and *Harlequin Historical Christmas
Stories*, we are proud to present FRIENDS, FAMILIES,
LOVERS. A collection of three new contemporary romance
stories about America at its best, about welcoming others into
the circle of love.... Stories to warm your heart ...

By three leading romance authors:

**KATHLEEN EAGLE
SANDRA KITT
RUTH JEAN DALE**

Available in October, wherever
Harlequin books are sold.

1993 Keepsake

CHRISTMAS

Stories

Capture the spirit and romance of Christmas with KEEPSAKE CHRISTMAS STORIES, a collection of three stories by favorite historical authors. The perfect Christmas gift!

Don't miss these heartwarming stories, available in November wherever Harlequin books are sold:

ONCE UPON A CHRISTMAS by Curtiss Ann Matlock
A FAIRYTALE SEASON by Marianne Willman
TIDINGS OF JOY by Victoria Pade

ADD A TOUCH OF ROMANCE TO YOUR HOLIDAY SEASON WITH KEEPSAKE CHRISTMAS STORIES!